THE FALLEN OF FOULWEATHER BLUFF

A THOMAS AUSTIN CRIME THRILLER,
BOOK 3

D.D. BLACK

DARKNESS AND LIGHT PUBLISHING

A Note on Setting

While many locations in this book are true to life, some details of the setting have been changed. Only one character in these pages exists in the real world: Thomas Austin's corgi, *Run*. Her personality mirrors that of my own corgi, Pearl. Any other resemblances between characters in this book and actual people is purely coincidental. In other words, I made them all up.

Thanks for reading,

D.D. Black

PART 1

SAND, MUD, AND MEDALS

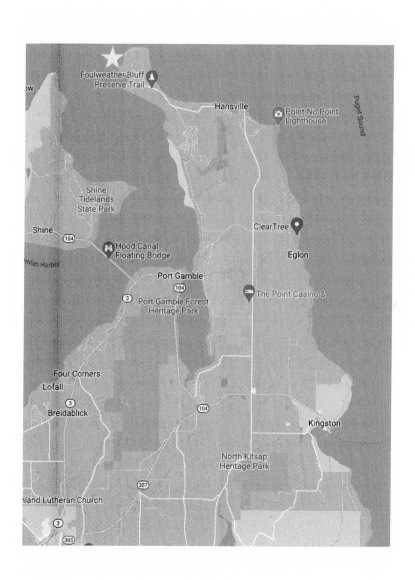

"Falsehood flies, and truth comes limping after it, so that when men come to be undeceived, it is too late; the jest is over, and the tale hath had its effect."
— Jonathan Swift

"The point of modern propaganda isn't only to misinform or push an agenda. It is to exhaust your critical thinking, to annihilate truth."
— Garry Kasparov

CHAPTER ONE

THE BROTHERS WERE FIGHTING AGAIN. They'd driven all the way out to Hansville to enjoy the beach on this gorgeous, late-spring day, but every time the families got together, Dimitri and Nikolai just *had* to ruin it.

Deena Fleck leaned on a large, barnacled rock, watching the children play in the shallow water of the tidepools. Up on the beach, her husband Dimitri scanned the sand with his metal detector, his older brother Nikolai strolling beside him talking about—actually *yelling* about—history, politics, and something called "Bitcoin," Dimitri's latest obsession.

Deena had walked down the beach to get away from them, preferring instead to watch the children play in the sand and marvel at the sea anemones and starfish. Only a fifteen minute walk from the road, Foulweather Bluff was a protected stretch of land that felt like it was at the edge of the world. She'd been to dozens of beaches in Kitsap County, but Foulweather Bluff was the only one she'd seen where the forest led almost all the way to the water. Not only that, the stunning marshlands ran right up to the forest edge, abutting both treeline and sandline.

"I think I found something!" Dimitri called.

She scanned up the beach, where her husband was on his knees, digging furiously. He always thought he'd find gold in the sand. Dimitri's optimism was one of the things she loved about him, but in ten years the most he'd found with that damn thing were a few quarters and a wedding ring someone lost in the sand. She'd made him leave the ring at the lost and found, which left the total income from the metal detector at seventy-five cents. They'd never see a return on what he liked to call, "the investment."

"What is it?" she called, walking over to him warily.

Thankfully, Nikolai had joined Emily further down the beach.

Dimitri's smile was intense, his breathing heavy. On his hands and knees, he looked like a kid ripping open the wrapping paper on the biggest box on Christmas morning.

"Could be anything," he said. "A rare silver dollar. A Rolex. Even gold coins. We might hit pay dirt. That's the magic. That's the mystery."

"Wonderful," she said sarcastically. "The magic and mystery of what is probably an empty beer can in the sand."

She tried not to mock her husband, but watching him dig like an excited puppy, she couldn't help it. He looked ridiculous in his glaring white shorts and t-shirt. A beige sun hat shaded his nose and cheeks, which he'd smeared with sunscreen but failed to rub in all the way. He looked like the cheesy dad from a vacation commercial.

"Here," he said. "I feel something."

All of a sudden he yanked something out of the sand and held it up. His smile dropped. He pulled his water bottle from his belt clip and poured a thin stream over the object, revealing a silver sheen. His lips curled. "It's a quarter."

"Great," Deena said. "Now we can take that trip to Paris we've been dreaming about."

He frowned and tossed a little sand at her bare legs. "You just wait. One day I'm gonna find something important."

Nikolai rejoined them from further down the beach. He was the taller of the two brothers, the richer of the two brothers and, by most standards, the handsomer of the two brothers. The only downside about Nikolai was that he was a complete jerk. "You find any Bitcoin in the sand, dumbass?"

Dimitri sighed. "Bitcoin is a *digital* currency, not a real coin. You just wait and see how rich I get."

Deena sighed. "Honey, he's mocking you."

Nikolai chuckled. "Always searching for easy money. Maybe try *working* for a living."

Dimitri returned to scanning the beach, working his way up the gentle slope that led away from the water toward the marshlands. Somehow his brother's mockery never bothered him for long. "You're trying to change the subject, brother, because you know I'm right about the Middle East."

Deena put her hands on her hips. "Look, you two. It's seventy degrees. Sunny. We just came out of a month straight of rain. Your kids are over there splashing in the waves." She pointed. "Remember them? Your *children*. Can you just enjoy it and stop arguing about nonsense?"

"Nonsense?" Dimitri asked, stepping over a large driftwood log as he worked further up the slope, his metal detector silent. "How is it nonsense? My idiot older brother says our wars are about oil. I say they're about freedom and—"

Beep Beep Beep. His metal detector went off again and, for an instant, Deena felt the excitement Dimitri always told her about. *What might be down there?*

The beeping grew louder and louder as he scanned back and forth. He stepped over another patch of driftwood, the beeping getting even louder. "There's stuff all over here," he said, his voice full of excitement.

Reaching the line where the sand met the damp marshland,

he settled over the spot with the loudest, most consistent beeping. Finally, he dropped to his knees. Deena couldn't help herself.
She hurried over and pecked him on the cheek. Sure he was a
fool sometimes, but he was *her* fool. As he shoved aside driftwood branches, she began digging, using her hands to scoop.

It didn't take long. In the cold, wet sand, her hand struck
something solid. Hard and cold. Metallic. Prying it out, she
pulled it into her line of sight. Round and rough, it was caked
with wet sand. An oversized coin, maybe.

"Please," Dimitri said. "Give it to me." His voice was soft, full
of wonder. He held out his hands as though she was holding a
delicate Faberge egg or a ticking bomb that had to be handled
with extreme caution.

She set it in his hand and he poured a thin stream of water onto
the object, washing away the sand. "A medal," he said, reverently.

"Hey, lemme see that," Nikolai had dropped down at his side.

Dimitri turned away, shielding his precious find.

The medal was dull bronze and marked with both words and
etched symbols or images.

"What does it say?" Deena asked.

Dimitri leaned in. "Um... Southwest Asia... Service Medal."

"Here!" Nikolai had been digging next to the spot where
Deena had pulled out the medal. "Found something else."

Dimitri poured water over the object in Nikolai's hand,
revealing another medal. Also bronze, this one was in the shape
of a cross. "Holy hell!" Nikolai said. "It's a Navy Cross."

Dimitri snatched it out of his brother's hand. "It's mine. I
found it. I..." He trailed off, studying the medal.

Nikolai said, "The Navy Cross is a big deal. Even though I
don't agree with the U.S. military, this is one of the highest
honors anyone can win. Do you think it's real?"

"Of course it's real," Dimitri said. He looked at Deena. "And
worth a *fortune*."

Deena wasn't sure about that, and something didn't feel right about this.

"But how would it have gotten here?" Nikolai asked.

The sun was hot on her neck. She stood, her insides roiling. Far down the beach, Nikolai's wife Emily looked up and Deena waved her over. Emily was older than all of them by a few years and the only one of the three who'd grown up in the area. More often than not, she was the voice of reason when the brothers' fights turned nasty.

As she walked over, Dimitri and Nikolai continued digging. Dimitri scanned the area as Nikolai, on his hands and knees, threw handfuls of sand to the side when they reached a spot that set off the metal detector. Over the next couple minutes, they pulled three more medals from the ground, repeating the process of cleaning them with the water bottle.

When Emily reached them, she ran a hand through her dark hair, looking concerned as she inspected their find. "Medals? Navy medals?"

"I'm gonna be rich," Dimitri said, dropping back to his knees to dig in another spot. "In total, I found three 'Southeast Asia Service' medals, one labeled 'Medal of Valor.' And the Navy Cross." He examined another find, then tossed it aside. "Just a bottle cap."

"*I* found the Navy Cross," Nikolai said. "But you're still an idiot. Medals aren't worth what you think. They're not real gold or anything."

"I bet they're worth—" Dimitri stopped suddenly. "I found something else." He'd been digging under the spot where he found the bottle cap. He pulled out something else, something larger.

Nikolai crowded in next to him and poured water on the object.

Emily gasped.

Deena stared in disbelief. It appeared to be a rounded bone fragment, stained from years in the muddy, sandy marshland.

"Is that..." Emily couldn't finish her sentence.

"I think it is," Deena said. Unless she was mistaken, it was a large section of skull. "Is... is that human?"

Dimitri and Nikolai exchanged glances, but, for the first time all afternoon, neither brother spoke.

Emily frowned at Deena. "I hope it's not what I think."

"What do you mean?" Deena asked. The look on Emily's face told her it was something bad, something worse than she could imagine.

"When I was ten years old, three Navy men disappeared. It was all over the newspapers, and everyone was talking about it. Memorial Day, 1992. They'd disappeared in full uniform, medals and all. One of them was a Navy Cross recipient. My parents couldn't stop talking about it. Last time they were seen alive they'd been drinking at the Watering Hole, which was what the little store in Hansville used to be called."

Dimitri looked crestfallen, but not because he might have discovered the bones of a dead man. "Will I be able to keep the medals?"

"You dumbass," Nikolai replied. "If Emily is right, this is a crime scene."

Dimitri spat in his brother's general direction, but didn't hit him. "I'm never giving them back. The medals are mine."

Deena felt sick to her stomach. She leveled her gaze at Emily. "You think this could be where... where they died? That someone buried them here? Medals and all?"

Emily nodded slowly.

Deena frowned at her husband. "Nikolai is right," she said. "We have to call the police."

CHAPTER TWO

THOMAS AUSTIN STARED at his phone nervously, then set it on the counter, promising himself he wouldn't check it again for another fifteen minutes. He wasn't the type to be on his phone all the time, but he was waiting for a message that could change everything.

His café was bustling this spring morning, the line for bait and beer stretching out the door toward the warm, sunny beach. After he and his kitchen crew had made it through the breakfast rush, he'd taken a seat at the counter and swiveled the stool to take in the scene. Every table was full of diners finishing plates of eggs and pancakes, drinking coffee, chatting, and looking happy. They'd made it through winter, and it was as though all of Hansville had come out to celebrate.

Austin felt a tap on his shoulder and turned back to the counter.

"Here it is." Andy set down a plate in front of him. "My latest culinary masterpiece."

Austin took in the dish. It was a breakfast sandwich roughly the size of his face, dripping with gooey cheese and glistening with maple syrup. "Okay, so it's bacon, a fried egg, sharp cheddar cheese, and maple syrup, right?"

Andy nodded. "And the 'bread' is malted waffles. I call it the I'm-Too-Sleepy-For-My-Fork. That's a reference from your generation, right?"

Austin looked at him blankly. Pop culture references weren't really his thing.

"You know. *Right Said Fred. I'm Too Sexy For My Shirt* or whatever. It's a nineties reference."

"What said who?"

Andy frowned. "You're hopeless. I'll show you the YouTube video when it's less busy."

The sandwich was more extravagant than anything Austin would have come up with, but he had to admit, it would look good on the Facebook page Andy had started to promote the business online. Though Austin still owned the joint and added recipes to the menu from time to time, he'd handed over the kitchen and day-to-day management of his café, general store, and bait shop to Andy. He'd also cut him in for ten percent of the profits, in addition to giving him another raise.

Austin bit into the sandwich. Salty, sweet, crispy and gooey, it was damn near a perfect bite of food. He didn't need to think hard. "Add it to the menu." He smiled while chewing. "And give yourself a raise."

"Will do." Andy walked back to the kitchen.

Austin glanced through the large windows to the beach, where small waves crashed on the shore, becoming white foam as the bright sun turned the water into a sea of sparkling sapphires. For the first time since moving to Hansville a year and a half earlier, Austin felt an optimism he couldn't quite explain.

It had been a long, gray winter. The rainiest April in anyone's memory. But May had come like a gift from the heavens—sunny, warm but not hot, with skies so clear and blue that Austin finally felt like he'd found his new forever home in Hansville. After a total overhaul of the tiny kitchen and Andy's promotion, Austin was free to spend more time fishing and digging into his only lead in the case of the murder of his wife, Fiona.

That's why he was waiting nervously for a message.

It had been a couple months since he'd learned that Fiona was involved in a top-secret drug case in New York City. He knew little other than the fact that it involved a man named Michael Lee. Problem was, he'd ended up finding ninety Michael Lees in New York City. He'd spent much of the last couple months emailing, calling, even writing actual letters on paper. But he'd gotten no closer to finding the right Michael Lee. Until yesterday.

That's when he'd received a postcard. The picture on the front was of a restaurant in Brooklyn, *Mama Dae's*. It had stopped Austin in his tracks. According to the short piece of writing Fiona had left behind when she died, Mama Dae's was the restaurant Michael Lee had gone to the night someone had tried to kill him. It wasn't much, but it was proof that one of the Michael Lees he'd contacted was the right one.

The card bore no return address. Only six words had been written in blocky, generic handwriting: DOWNLOAD THE SIGNAL APP AND WAIT.

One of the many Michael Lees he'd reached out to had decided to reach back. So early that morning, Austin had down-loaded Signal—which he'd learned was an end-to-end encrypted messaging app.

He flipped over his phone and checked the app for a message. Nothing.

When he'd told his friend Detective Ridley that he finally had a lead after eighteen months, Ridley told him, "Hope ain't a lead. Hope is what's *leading* you."

Austin had to admit he was right. Michael Lee wasn't much of a lead, but Austin had hope again, and, for now, that was enough. Things would never be what they were—he'd never stop grieving—but late spring and summer in western Washington were too beautiful to ignore, and hope was something that had been in short supply lately.

"It's too runny!" A little girl's shrieking voice broke his reveries. "And the bacon's too hard. And why can't we go to the beach!" At the table behind him, his best customers—Mr. and Mrs. McGuillicutty—sat with their granddaughter.

Austin turned as Mrs. McGuillicutty tried to quiet the little girl. "Foulweather Bluff isn't the *only* beach. We'll find another after we eat."

"I want something else!" the little girl continued.

Austin crossed the café and took the fourth seat at their table.

"I'm sorry," Mr. McGuillicutty said. "She's fussy." He turned to the girl, who looked to be six or seven. "This is the owner of the café, Olivia. Don't insult him."

Austin waved a hand. "It's okay." He took the plate, leaning in and examining it as though looking through a magnifying glass. "Now let me see here. Hmmm, yes, the egg does look a *little* runny and the bacon is a *shade* darker than it ought to be." He set the plate down. "As a former NYPD detective, I must get to the bottom of this!"

The little girl looked surprised, almost stunned. "It's okay. I was... uhhh..."

"Tell you what," Austin said, grabbing his plate from the counter. He cut the waffle sandwich in half, then looked to Mrs. McGuillicutty for approval. She nodded.

"While I interview suspects about why your eggs are runny and your bacon overcooked, how about you try our newest menu item, the... *what'd you call it?*" Austin called to Andy, who was delivering a plate to a nearby diner.

Andy looked up. "I'm-Too-Sleepy-For-My-Fork."

"Yes," Austin said. "Introducing the I'm-Too-Sleepy-For-My-Fork sandwich."

Olivia laughed. "Hey, I'm not sleepy."

"But you do love waffles. And you *really* love syrup." He smiled. "I've seen you here before. The last time you ordered waffles you caused an international maple syrup shortage."

She laughed again and looked to her grandma for permission. Mrs. McGuillicutty nodded.

Olivia bit into the sandwich and smiled. "It's good," she managed through a mouthful of food.

"On the house," Austin said, taking her other plate back to the kitchen.

He and Fiona had been talking about having children in the months before she died. The older he got, the more he regretted not having any of his own. And, as his mother loved to point out every time the subject arose, he wasn't getting any younger.

He found his corgi, Run, curled up in the sun just outside the door that led from the kitchen to the parking lot. He scraped the egg off the plate into her bowl. She leapt up and inhaled it in two giant bites, then studied him for a moment and lay down again.

The familiar sound of car tires over gravel made him look up. A white SUV pulled into the lot and, for a moment, he thought it was Anna Downey, the local crime reporter with whom he'd worked a couple cases lately. They'd also shared a flirtation and one date, which was a disaster entirely of his own making.

But it wasn't Anna. This was a larger SUV marked with the shield of NCIS—the Naval Criminal Investigative Service. And it certainly wasn't Anna who got out of the driver's seat. This woman wore blue jeans and a white collared shirt under a black vest, also marked with the NCIS shield. Her jet black hair glistened in the bright sun and, for a moment, he thought she must be lost. Then he saw Detective Calvin Ridley ease out of the passenger seat and join her as she walked toward the café.

Austin respected Ridley because he led his team of detectives the way Austin would have had he stayed in the NYPD. Tough but fair, leading by example, and always willing to step up and take the blame for his team when things didn't go according to plan. But what was he doing in Hansville with an NCIS agent?

Austin met them halfway across the parking lot. If the presence of an NCIS agent in the sleepy beach town wasn't enough to tell him something was up, the look on Ridley's face did the trick. "Ridley, to what do I owe this visit?"

"Austin, this is Symone Aoki, Special Agent of the Major Case Response Team from NCIS."

Austin shook her extended hand. She looked him up and down as though assessing him, but didn't smile. She was only a little shorter than Austin, maybe five-foot-ten, and stood straight-backed but not stiff, shoulders upright and squared. Austin thought she looked like someone who knew her way around a firearm. "Call me Sy. Ridley tells me you're the local I should speak with."

"If he meant speak with about bait, or our new waffle sandwich, then yeah." He looked from Sy to Ridley, then back to Sy. "But I'm guessing that's not why you're here."

She shook her head and held a plastic baggie in front of Austin's face. The bright sun illuminated what looked to be four or five Navy medals. He recognized the Navy Cross right away. "I know you wouldn't be showing those to me if something *good* had happened."

Ridley frowned. "You hear about the Memorial Day disappearance of 1992?"

Austin shook his head.

Sy said, "Three decorated Navy men, officers, all young. Disappeared on Memorial Day 1992. Multiple investigations, a few suspects, but nothing ever came of it. Case was colder than an ice cube in a snowstorm."

Austin took the baggie, examining the medals. In addition to the Navy Cross, there was a Medal of Valor and three Southwest Asia Service Medals, issued to men and women who served in the Gulf War in the early nineties. "I'm guessing the case just warmed up," Austin said, handing the baggie back to Sy.

"These medals were found at Foulweather Bluff. Along with the bones—some of the bones—of the men. We have a crew there right now."

"That's why the Bluff has been closed off for a couple days?" Austin asked. "Figured it was a downed tree or something."

Ridley ran a hand over his bald head. His temples popped. Last time Austin had seen him, he'd been over the moon, waxing philosophical about life. His wife Rachel was pregnant again. Now he looked five years older and a hundred times more stressed. Ridley was the type of detective who thrived on tough cases, but not on publicity. Austin hadn't heard about this case, but he could already tell it was going to be a big one.

Ridley let out a long sigh, like a tea kettle releasing steam. "We think all the April rain and wind washed the bodies up, dislodged the medals. Buried in the marsh for thirty years."

Austin let his head fall back enough for the sun to hit his eyes and warm his face. Something in the pit of his stomach dropped, and he tasted tart cherries and burnt toast. His synesthesia had been triggered in a new way.

Tart cherries always meant curiosity, the excitement of a new case. He loved the unknown. But the burnt toast flavor was dread. Something about this case scared him.

He knew what was coming next.

Ridley said, "Can we go inside your apartment and chat? We're hoping you can help us out."

CHAPTER THREE

"LET ME START BY SAYING, I don't want to be here." Sy sat next to Ridley, frowning at Austin as though it was somehow *his* fault she'd come to see him.

Her demeanor had changed since they'd come into his apartment. Outside she'd been cool, but professional. Now that they were alone, she'd gone from cool to cold.

"Then why *are* you here?" Austin asked.

Sy folded her hands in her lap, considering this. "You know much about the Navy?"

Austin nodded at the picture of his mom on the wall, wearing her uniform. "I never served, but I'm a Navy brat. Around it my whole life."

Sy glanced at the picture. "Then you'll understand that sometimes we get orders to do things we don't want to do, that we don't think are necessary." She sighed, irritated. "We do them anyway."

"*A Few Good Men*," Ridley said. "'We follow orders or people die. It's that simple.'"

Austin frowned. People always referenced that film when they learned his mother was a JAG lawyer.

"Understood," Austin said to Sy. "I guess I'm wondering what you've been ordered to do."

Sy pulled a brown folder from her handbag. "Before we get into that, I'd like to tell you a little bit about the situation."

Austin nodded.

"Memorial Day, 1992." Sy's voice was all business. "Three men —all Naval officers—are drinking at the Watering Hole, which is what your café used to be called, apparently. It was more of a bar back then. Adam Del Guado, age 26. Jack Hammeron, age 28— everyone called him 'Hammer'—and the youngster, Joey Blake, age 24. That day, they'd been part of a ceremony at the local cemetery, honoring a member of their squad who'd been lost in Desert Storm. They were all in uniform. Medals, everything. After the ceremony, they went to the Watering Hole. Left around nine o'clock and were never seen again."

As she spoke, something jostled loose from Austin's memory. "I didn't know their names or even that they were in Hansville when they disappeared, but I remember this. We were on the east coast when it happened. Connecticut. My mother was quite upset. Followed the case closely."

Sy frowned. "*Everyone* was upset about it."

She had an odd demeanor. Formal, to the point. At first Austin had thought she was upset at *him*, but the more she spoke, the more she appeared upset by the case and the fact that she'd been ordered to do something she didn't think would help resolve it. He had to admit, there was something he liked about her.

He never intended to compare anyone to Fiona, but sometimes he couldn't help it. And in Sy he was reminded of his wife's all-business demeanor, bordering on frigidity, that—for some reason—he found attractive.

Sy crossed and uncrossed her legs, seemingly growing more irritated by the minute. "For NCIS and the Navy, this case was a *huge* failure. One of the biggest unsolved cases in Navy history.

Got re-opened in 2011. Another year of work went into it, and nothing."

"The men?" Austin asked. "What can you tell me about them?"

Sy stood, laced her hands behind her back, and examined the photographs on his wall. She moved with a precision and formality that was both appealing and unnerving.

"Best of the best," Ridley said. "That Navy Cross wasn't a Halloween prop."

Sy agreed. "Medals were found by a family with a metal detector. Hammer got the Navy Cross. Medal of Valor to Adam Del Guado. But all three had exceptional service records. Joey Blake was younger, but on the fastest track." She turned. "Notes in his records are so glowing, Blake might be *running* the Navy right now if he hadn't died."

Austin nodded gravely. "You said 'died.' I'm assuming you found more than medals?"

Sy nodded, meeting his eyes. "Bones." She held his gaze, and her eyes were so dark they were almost black. He didn't know why, but he felt as though she had a deep well of pain inside that was similar to his own.

He looked at the floor. Hearing about fallen soldiers was terrible. Hearing that they were the best the Navy had to offer, and their deaths remained unsolved, hit him like a painful itch he couldn't scratch. He tasted dry sand.

Run bolted in from the kitchen, where she'd been chewing the dehydrated pig's ear Austin had given her. She sniffed Sy's shoes curiously, then licked Ridley's hand. Then she went to the middle of the room and collapsed into a sploot, belly down with her back legs splayed out behind her. She soaked up the cool from the floor, studying the strangers in her home from afar.

"Right now," Sy continued, "MCRT is over at Foulweather Bluff. There's nothing I want more than to be over there with them."

"Which I imagine brings you to why you don't want to be here," Austin said.

"Look, it's not your fault, Thomas. Or is it Austin?"

He smiled, trying to sound friendly. "Austin, like the wrestler, or the Six Million Dollar Man."

She nodded politely. "It's not your fault, Austin. This case is important. Beyond important. It's rare we get something that looks like a homicide. And rarer that it's a triple, and even rarer that it's a well-known cold case." She paused. "Actually, it's not rare. It's unique."

Ridley sighed, eyeing Austin. "This case is one of one."

"So," Sy continued, "I've been ordered by people above me to get another view. Someone outside NCIS. We're working with locals, like Ridley here."

Austin held up a hand to stop her. "Why isn't that enough? I mean, he's outside the Navy, outside NCIS."

She looked from Austin to Ridley, then back to Austin. "Okay, I wasn't ordered to find *someone* outside NCIS. I was ordered to consult you. *You* specifically."

Austin was confused. Had he heard that right? "Me? Who ordered that?"

She stood, cocked her head, and gave him a look that told him there was no way she would answer, even if she could.

His mind spun like a wobbly top. Who in NCIS could have wanted Sy to consult with him? "I've only lived here a year and a half. Barely anyone knows I live here."

Ridley stood. "Look, Austin. You know she can't say much. Give us the day, show Sy the peninsula, come out to the scene at the Bluff. It'll be fun."

Austin raised an eyebrow. "Fun?" Since Ridley had found out his wife was pregnant, he'd been in a happy, philosophical mood that contrasted with his linebacker size and severe, serious face.

"Sorry," Ridley said. "Not fun. Interesting. Important. I know you're curious."

Austin tried to get a read on Sy, who'd taken his back and forth with Ridley as an opportunity to check her phone. She looked disinterested, like a teenager working retail just waiting for her shift to end.

But Ridley was right. He *was* curious. And not only about Jack Hammeron, Adam Del Guado, and Joey Blake. He was curious why Sy was acting so strange, and who had asked her to consult with him.

"I'll drive," Austin said. "Anyone else want a coffee for the road?"

CHAPTER FOUR

"SO HOW DID a former NYPD detective end up out here?" Sy cracked the window, filling the car with a perfect Hansville breeze. Clean and cool, cedar trees and salt air.

Austin didn't reply.

Ridley had offered her shotgun, cramming himself into the back seat of Austin's truck.

Sy cleared her throat. "I'm sorry. Ridley told me about your wife. I know what happened. But why Hansville?"

"It's alright," Austin said. "I lived in Bremerton for a bit as a kid. When I decided to move, I thought, how far away from New York City can I get? Then I heard about the café being for sale and, well, I wanted to perfect my lobster ravioli recipe. It all happened fast." He smiled and gestured out the window at the scenery. "I wasn't in my right mind, but sometimes that leads to good decisions."

They'd been touring the peninsula for ten minutes, Austin taking them south from his store, briefly veering east through Point No Point where, not long ago, he'd helped take down a serial killer. It was odd revisiting the place. It had been one of his favorite beaches and was still one of the most popular attractions in the area. But it would never feel the same. Sy had asked smart questions—both about the area in general and what had gone down around Christmas, which she'd read about in the papers. Austin had told her all he knew about the area, Ridley filling in when his knowledge flagged.

From Hansville Road they turned west through Little Boston, then hit the other side of the peninsula and turned onto Hood Canal Drive. Heading north, they crossed a series of speed tables and turns, including a hairpin that angled down sharply and looked as though it might drop them off the cliff onto the beach below. Every turn offered a new, dramatic view of mountains, trees, sky, and water.

Sy held up the coffee cup Austin had given her. "It's good. Not too dark, not too light."

Austin looked at her, surprised at the compliment. Her tone had lightened, and he wasn't sure why. "We get it from a roaster in Seattle twice a week."

"The scenery—the water, the beaches, the trees. I can see why you moved here." She sipped her coffee.. "I'm sorry I was rude before. It's just... this isn't how I saw my first huge case going."

"Understood," Austin said. "It might help if—"

"Don't ask who told me to contact you."

Austin rolled down his window and pointed toward the water. "This is the west side of the Peninsula. Marina down there. Driftwood Keys. Swimming pool, playground, beach area. Foulweather Bluff isn't far. So you've never been here?"

"Once," she said. "And..." She trailed off. "Look, I was being a jerk before. It's not because of you, and it's not because of the case. Well, it's a little because of the case. NCIS isn't like on TV. We don't get a sensational new case every episode. The victims in this case were heroes. Solving this would be huge for me, and would make all the BS I deal with worth it."

Austin sensed there was more. "You said you'd been here once?"

"With my husband." She blinked. "Weird memories."

Austin didn't know how to take this. "Okay?"

"He passed away in a submarine accident. Four years ago. He was a Navy Diver. A welder."

Even though he tried to keep abreast of the news out of the Navy, and his mother filled him in from time to time, he didn't recall hearing about the accident. But it made her strange demeanor make more sense. "I'm sorry," he said.

They drove in silence, each looking out the window. Austin turned onto Twin Spits Road, heading west toward Foulweather Bluff. He knew better than anyone that "I'm sorry" wasn't enough, but sometimes it was all there was.

"I don't even remember why we were here," Sy said. "Wasn't a special occasion or anything. Maybe he had a friend out here—a BBQ or something. It's weird, the stuff you remember. Hadn't thought about this town for years. Then we show up and all of a sudden memories start flooding in. When we came down the hill into town and I saw the water and then Whidbey Island in the distance, it was like a deja vu, and then..."

"You don't have to say anything more," Austin said. "I understand."

"I never met him," Ridley said, "but Sheriff Daniels told me he was the best diver the Navy had."

"Thanks," Sy said. She turned to look at Ridley, whose knees were pressed up around his chin in the back seat. "I should have given you the front."

"Don't worry about it. Wanted you to have the view."

"Your wife?" Sy asked. "She's how far along?"

"Five months."

"She..." Sy's voice cracked and went quiet as Austin stopped his truck along the side of the road and shut off the engine. "Just make sure she knows you love her."

"I do," Ridley said.

As Austin opened the door, he stopped suddenly. His mouth was full of the taste of... what? It was like all the umami flavors—mushrooms, seaweed, steak, and miso—almost like the taste of the rich earth itself but in viscous form, like they had been steeped in oil. He watched Sy get out, then waited for Ridley to spring himself loose from the back seat. His synesthesia had never manifested in this way, and he had no words for the emotion. He stared up at the little patch of blue sky visible between two evergreens. The only way he could describe the feeling was like if the weight of history had been brought into the present moment. He thought of Fiona, of Sy losing her husband in a random accident, of Ridley and his wife expecting a new child. It was as though history and the unrelenting movement of time had taken on weight and settled in him.

"Austin?" Ridley said. "What's wrong?"

He shook his head, trying to come back to the moment, then waved Ridley and Sy under the yellow police tape strung between trees at the head of the trail. He couldn't dwell on it, and didn't want to talk about it.

A little way down the trail, Austin ducked under a low-hanging branch. "Half a mile or so. The beach is protected, so no pets, no way to get there except this little path." What he was thinking, but didn't say, was that it was a good place to murder someone. It was remote, and, because the beach was surrounded by marshlands, it wasn't lined with homes like many of the local beaches. Even on beautiful summer days, he rarely saw more than a few people here, though he didn't come often because Run wasn't allowed.

Sy stopped, leaning on a mossy cedar tree. "I've read the original case, as well as the file from when this thing got re-opened." She let her head fall back, taking in the canopy of evergreen branches above her. "Why the hell would three of our best Navy men be out here that night to begin with? And how could someone manage to kill all three of them?"

Ridley stepped around her on the path. "That's what I've been wondering. All three of them were more than capable of handling themselves. For one person to take them all out... it's not impossible, obviously, but not likely. Of course, the case files don't say anything about how they were murdered. Maybe we find out today."

They continued up the path. "Do you have *anything* yet on cause of death?" Austin asked. "Bullets, evidence of violence, or only the medals?"

"Nothing yet. We've got a whole team there now," Sy said. "You'll know when I know."

The undergrowth thickened and then suddenly the water came into view between two trees. Sy passed him, leading the way off the bluff and onto the beach. The area with all the activity was only a hundred yards from the end of the trail, a spot where the grassy marshlands met the beach at a line of driftwood. More police tape had been set up, stretched between stakes stuck into the ground and marking off an area half a football field in size. Inside the tape, about half a dozen people were working.

As they made their way up to the police tape, a team of two men and one woman approached. Austin stayed a couple paces behind, content to listen in.

"Austin and Ridley," Sy said, "this is the dream team. Marty Greelish, forensic dentist. Sandra O'Cleary, forensic anthropologist, and David Blowenstein, forensic pathologist."

Austin shook their hands, but they quickly turned their attention back to Sy. It was Blowenstein who spoke first. "The night these three men died was unseasonably cold. Low forties in May. I looked it up." Blowenstein was in his mid-forties, like Austin, but had a baby face and spoke like he was on stage, as though projecting to try to reach someone out on the water.

Greelish, the forensic dentist, let out a quiet sigh and mumbled, "Here we go," under his breath. He was older, with black glasses and short gray hair that matched his goatee. Austin could sense a rivalry.

Blowenstein waved him off. "I say that because we're hoping to find clothing, a synthetic fiber jacket or something of the sort, something that might have lasted thirty years. So far, nothing."

"But we have bones," O'Cleary chirped. "Oh yes, we have *bones*." She had a bright Irish accent and spoke as though she was describing a special dessert to a child.

Blowenstein smiled. "We have bones, indeed."

Austin had seen this before. These folks didn't get out of the lab much and might only work a handful of cases like this in an entire career. Still, he found their excitement off-putting. After all, they were digging through the sand and mud to find the remains of three dead soldiers.

"Cut the BS," Sy barked. "Tell me what you have."

Greelish adjusted his glasses. "Teeth from all three men. 99.99% certainty. All the stuff these two will spew at you in the next few minutes may or may not be true. One thing we know: the three missing Navy men are dead, and their bodies all ended up here."

Austin nodded at him. He liked a man who offered up the facts without a lot of embellishment.

"You're no fun," O'Cleary said to him. "I—"

"If I may," Blowenstein interjected.

"You may *not*!" O'Cleary said. She was about half Blowenstein's size and sounded like an angry leprechaun. "You shouldn't even *be* here. What the horses arse good is a pathologist going to do when all we have are bone and teeth fragments?"

"I studied crime scenes and—"

"I'm only going to say this once," Sy said, raising a finger to silence them. "Bury your damn egos in the sand right now." She jabbed the finger in Blowenstein's direction before he could object. "Silence."

Looking at O'Cleary, Sy said, "Facts only. Go."

O'Cleary cleared her throat. "Skull fragments we believe to be from three different men. Two with evidence of bullet entry, though I can only say that with about sixty percent certainty at this point. Will know more soon. Multiple other bone fragments. Some animal—deer, raccoon—but definitely human as well. Shoulder blade from a male definitely chipped consistent with a bullet wound, but—it's been thirty years—I'm never going to be able to give you the certainty he can." She nodded in the dentist's direction, then looked at the ground and stepped back.

"Thank you," Sy said, turning to Blowenstein.

Austin scanned the beach, trying to imagine a scenario by which three men got taken out here. It was also quite possible, he realized, that they hadn't been killed here at all. Perhaps they'd been killed elsewhere, even individually, then brought here by the killer to hide the bodies.

Blowenstein said, "Without fresh bodies, everything we say—other than Greelish's tooth stuff—is going to involve some speculation. Can't say a lot about firing distance. No skin markings to study. No contact wounds. Gas deposits. Soot. We've got none of it."

"I know what you *don't* have," Sy said, impatiently. "Tell me what you *do* have."

"There's some good news and..." Blowenstein grew serious... "We should have led with this because it likely proves that the men were killed here, not simply left here after death. Bullet casings. Rifle. Typical twenty-two cal. Three so far, but I bet we find more. And we just found this." He held up a tiny plastic baggie.

Austin shifted his head to allow the sun to illuminate the bullet casing inside.

It was like nothing he'd ever seen.

CHAPTER FIVE

SY TOOK the baggie and examined it, then handed it to Austin. The bullet was steel, with an odd brass base and a hollow rear.

"Who the hell uses this sort of bullet?" Sy asked.

"What sort *is* it?" Austin asked, handing the baggie to Ridley.

"Russians," Ridley said, speaking for the first time. "Fifty years ago." Like Austin, he'd chosen to hang back and listen. After all, this was Sy's show.

Blowenstein nodded. "And collectors. Or just weirdos."

"7.62mm," Ridley said. "I can't remember which, but it was designed for some Soviet-era experimental pistol. A crappy weapon, it turned out, but this caseless design was something they tried."

"Where was it found in relation to the rifle bullets?" Sy asked.

Blowenstein pointed to a log about forty yards down the beach. "Further away. And if I might..." he ducked his large frame under the police tape and led them to the log. "I have a theory. And, I do mean, *theory*. All the medals and bones were found in the same spot, further up, closer to the marsh. This bullet was found here."

Sy looked at O'Cleary. "Any way to tell if one of these bullets killed one of our victims?"

O'Cleary shook her head. "Not likely. Back in the lab we'll do the analysis, but I'm not hopeful. The bones just don't have enough markings to be conclusive about anything."

Blowenstein said, "My theory is that one of the men was killed down here with the pistol that matches this rare bullet. Then maybe the shooter was dragging him into the marshlands to hide the body and came across the other two men, or they came across him."

Sy looked skeptical. "Then killed them with a *different* weapon?"

"It's not much," Blowenstein admitted.

"Like I said when you arrived," Greelish said, running a hand over his goatee, "all we know for sure is that we have the teeth of three dead men. The rest is just storytelling."

Back at his café, Austin walked Sy and Ridley across the parking lot, stopping at Sy's SUV.

"Any thoughts?" she asked, leaning against the door.

"Not many," Austin said. "I mean, you don't have much."

"This is a black box," Ridley said. "I don't envy you. That bullet is something to look into, but old Soviet-era ammunition flooded the market toward the end of the Cold War." He thought for a moment, running a hand over his bald head. "Although I don't think they made a ton of that type. I don't know. Something to look into."

Sy nodded and turned to Austin. "I won't be in touch about the case—my promise went only so far as to include you in the initial visit and to get the lay of the land..." She gave him an odd look. "But I'll be in touch about those ravioli."

Austin was confused. He looked from Sy to Ridley, then back to Sy.

"You said you came here to perfect the recipe," Sy said. "I've heard they're good." And with that, she opened the door and slid into the driver's seat.

Ridley raised an eyebrow in Austin's general direction, then followed her into the car.

He watched them pull away, wondering whether she'd been flirting. He honestly wasn't sure how to tell anymore. Between her rapidly-shifting attitude and the once-in-a-lifetime case that he'd been brought into briefly, it had been an odd morning.

As he approached the door of his café, a familiar voice hit him from the shadows. "Who was that?"

It was Anna Downey. She was sitting in a wooden chair at one of the two outdoor tables Austin had set out facing the water.

"No one," Austin said. "I mean, Ridley, and..."

"Weird, I didn't know that Ridley and 'No one' were friends. Interesting." She was pretending to be more upset than she was, but she was definitely somewhere between irked and annoyed.

Austin sat in the empty seat next to her. "I can't say."

Anna frowned. "Something to do with the fact that Foul-weather Bluff is closed?"

Austin said nothing.

"You hearing any grumblings out of the naval base? I'm hearing some things."

Again, Austin didn't reply.

"And who was that woman with Ridley? I mean, NCIS obviously, but what was her name?"

"Are you ever *not* working on a story?"

She shook her head. "You know anyone there I can talk to? I mean, I have sources, but I can always use better ones."

Her tone was less friendly than it had been up until their

failed date. He'd seen her once or twice since, but she'd gotten more formal and had definitely stopped showing an interest in a romantic relationship. He couldn't blame her. She'd cooked him a special dinner and he'd been too obsessed with a minor development in his investigation into Fiona's murder to appreciate it.

A green Chevy Malibu pulled up and Anna recoiled. "Oh no."

"What?"

"I think that's... yup. Davey Wragg. Oh, God."

A tall, thin man emerged from the car, walking with long strides toward the front door of the café. When he saw them, he changed course, ignoring Austin and stopping in front of Anna. "As I live and breathe."

His jeans were loose and filthy, his white t-shirt mostly hidden by a green hooded sweatshirt. Greasy threads of light brown hair peeked out under his blue Mariners cap.

"Davey. How are you?" Anna didn't make eye contact.

"Better now," he said. "Why didn't you call me back?"

Finally, she looked up. "I'm sorry about that. It wasn't a good match. I should have just said that."

He pulled a plastic toothpick from his pocket and began gnawing on it. He still hadn't so much as glanced at Austin, but Austin recognized him. He'd been in the store at least a couple times.

"Miller Lite?" Austin said, trying to break the icy silence. "I think I sold you a case of Miller Lite once."

Wragg glanced at him. "Maybe." He turned slightly, angling between Austin and Anna. "You *should have* called me back."

"I'm in the middle of something," Anna said, flatly.

"Woman who don't call me back are—"

Anna stood abruptly. "First of all, it's 'women.' And second of all, don't threaten me."

He licked his dry, cracked lips. "I like an angry women. Gives me something to *subdue*." He leaned in, stooping to get right in

Anna's face. She tried to shove him away, but he pressed in like he was trying to force her back into the chair.

In one motion, Austin stood while swinging his right arm forward, grasping Wragg's wrist and twisting it behind his back, just to the point where it would hurt like hell but not break.

Wragg squirmed, trying to go with the direction of the twist, and pulled free as he fell into the gravel parking lot. He leapt up quicker than Austin would have thought he could in those baggy jeans.

"That was a mistake," Wragg said, his voice hard but not especially intimidating.

"The mistake," Anna said, shoving Austin out of the way, "was me ever going out with you to begin with."

Wragg licked his lips again, looking at Anna as though he'd forgotten Austin was there. What the hell was wrong with this guy? Besides the fact that he said "woman" when he meant "women," and vice versa, he had a demeanor that was almost menacing, but it was too strange, too unbelievable, as though he only barely knew what he was doing.

In any case, Austin had seen enough.

With three strides, he was chest-to-chest with Wragg. "Do you know who I am?"

"That easterner who bought the store." He licked his lips. "You come across the country to bang our woman out here?"

Austin grabbed the hood of his sweatshirt, which was the same forest green as his Chevy, and dragged him across the parking lot, Wragg kicking his legs in the gravel.

Austin yanked open the car door, swinging it into Wragg's head, hard enough to hurt but gentle enough not to knock him out, then shoved him into the driver's seat. "Don't ever set foot on my property again. You're banned for life." He leaned in until he was nose to nose with the guy, until he could smell the stale cigarettes on his breath. "And if you ever contact Anna again."

He shook his head as though he couldn't even describe what he would do to him. "*Don't* ever call her again."

He slammed the door so hard he thought it might shatter the window. Then he stepped aside and stared at Wragg, who was checking his head in the rearview mirror for blood.

Austin kept staring until Wragg pulled out of his parking lot, then he returned to the store.

"You see why I wanted to go out with you?" Anna said. "That's the kind of guy the dating apps were matching me with."

"It's nothing to joke about," Austin said. "Are you alright?"

She nodded and they walked inside. Some of the patrons had left their tables to gawk at the commotion, staring out the large picture windows that faced the parking lot.

"That guy's been a pain in our ass around here since he was a little kid," Mr. McGuillicutty said. Apparently they'd taken little Olivia back to her parents, then come back to his café for lunch.

"Peed on my tulips when he was nine years old," Mrs. McGillicutty added.

"Sorry for that," Anna said as they sat down at the counter. "Went out with him one time a year ago. We connected on one of those crappy dating apps. Besides being broke, he creeped me out on multiple levels. And trust me, his profile picture did *not* look like that."

"No need to apologize." Austin was still a little shaken. He'd never had to kick anyone out of his store, never had a run in like that with a customer. "He live here?"

"We met out at a restaurant. But yeah, somewhere back in the woods. Can we change the subject?"

"Sure, unless it's back to who the woman with Ridley was, and why Foulweather Bluff is closed."

She waved a hand. "I'll get that from someone else."

"Deal."

Austin's phone vibrated and he recognized Ridley's number.

Excusing himself, he walked across the parking lot toward the beach, letting the bright sun warm his face. "Rid?"

"Austin, Sy just dropped me off at my car. Something's up."

"Was she flirting with me?" Austin surprised himself by coming right out with it.

"She was, but believe it or not, that's *not* why I'm calling."

Austin chuckled. "Sorry, it's just... I've lost the ability to tell. I'm listening."

"Sy got a call on the way back. Let it go to voicemail but it was a blocked number. Pulled over and had me get out. Called someone. After that, she clammed up. Said, 'Thanks for everything,' as though we were done."

"Okay, but it's her case, right?"

"It's more her case than mine, but it's mine too. Overlapping jurisdictions. I sent you an email."

Austin noticed Anna watching him, possibly eavesdropping, and took a few more steps toward the beach. "Whoa whoa whoa. Sent me what?"

"Files."

"From the case? *This* case? I'm not supposed to have those."

"But I am," Ridley said. "And you're hired."

"Hired for what?"

"Seems like Sy is writing off my department. Doesn't mean I have to write back."

"Huh?"

"Not sure what she's up to," Ridley said, "but I have every right to pursue my own investigation. Whether she likes it or not, this went from a cold missing persons case to a murder investigation in my county."

Austin had a hundred objections. "But—"

"Yeah yeah yeah. I've heard your objections before, Austin. Not this time."

He didn't feel comfortable having the files, but technically it was Ridley who'd overstepped by sending them to him. What harm could it do to take a peek?

"Spend an hour or two with the files," Ridley continued, "and I have no doubt you'll be all in."

Austin was already opening the email on his phone. "I'll be in touch."

CHAPTER SIX

*Buy a new laptop from a store you've never visited. Download the TOR browser. Get a VPN. Download the Invisible Video App. Create a user-name. Send a message to username **ghrpdhal784hfjal**, then wait. Do not reply to this message. Don't call me again. Ever. You almost got me killed.*

IT WAS 5 AM and Austin had already read the message three times. It was only yesterday that he had downloaded the encrypted Signal messaging app, and he'd already heard from the mysterious messenger he assumed was Michael Lee.

After staying up late reading through the files Ridley had sent him, he'd woken up to Run licking his face, then rolled over in bed to find a new notification. The message had arrived in the middle of the night.

He didn't understand what was going on, but he was certain he would follow the instructions to the letter. But as bad as he was with tech, he'd need some help.

Opening a new message, he tapped out a text to Ridley.

I read through some of the files. Will keep going on one condition: allow me to 'borrow' Samantha for a small job, with her permission. I'll pay her. It's a computer thing I need help with. Don't want to say more, but I promise it won't get her in any trouble.

To his surprise, Ridley texted back right away.

Fine, as long as she agrees, and it's off my clock. Call me after you've had more time with the files. Not everything from the original investigation got scanned in, or, at least, I didn't get them all before Sy stopped sharing.

Austin walked into the kitchen and poured himself a cup of cold coffee, still in the pot from the day before. He drank it in three big gulps, then put on a fresh pot and called his mom.

"Austin, it's early out there."

"I always get up this early." He opened the door and tossed a tennis ball into the yard. Run bolted after it and returned a moment later. Despite her thick, low-to-the-ground body, she was fast as lightning. "How's dad?"

He could hear the TV on in the background and, as always, it was playing cable news way too loudly. "Worse than ever."

His parents still lived back east, where his mom took care of his dad, who was in year three of the long goodbye. He'd been diagnosed with Alzheimer's before Fiona died, and things had only grown harder on his mother since. Austin figured it was hard on his dad as well, but they hadn't had much of a conversation in years. His dad had been a big soccer fan and still remembered specific goals scored in World Cup matches from before Austin was born, but he usually didn't remember his own son. It made Austin feel helpless and vaguely guilty that there was nothing he could do.

"Any good moments?" Austin asked.

"We had our share before," his mother said flatly. "This is the price we pay." He could hear her footsteps on the wooden floor. She'd always paced when speaking on the phone.

Austin tossed the ball again. "There's something I want to ask you about."

"Triple homicide?"

Austin knelt to grab the ball from Run, who had already returned. "How'd you know?"

"The disappearance of those boys was a big deal. Word gets around. It's remarkable that they found their remains. The medals."

Austin paused, holding the soggy tennis ball between his thumb and forefinger. "Wait, word gets around *how*, specifically?"

"Captain Luke Seymour Garrison."

The name rang a bell, but Austin couldn't place it. "He is..."

"Executive Officer at Bremerton. We worked together on some things way back when."

"Any chance you told him to get me involved in this thing?"

Run barked, and Austin threw the ball for her, then went inside. Run retrieved it, then followed at his heels.

"Me? Ask him?" His mother sounded surprised. "No. I only heard about it last night. He mentioned you might be involved is all. I'd been ignoring his calls for a few days, and finally gave in and answered. He used to have a thing for me."

Austin wanted to cover his ears. His mother had always been more open about relationship talk than he or his father.

She cleared her throat. "But that's so exciting. It's an important case."

"There's an interesting woman from NCIS named Symone Aoki. She asked for my help, sort of. Then... well... I'm not entirely sure what's going on, but I'm not sure I want to get involved. I have a feeling this one could get bleak. The Navy has a weight to it, a gravity. It pulls everything in and sometimes—"

"They never get out. I know. You don't have to tell me about the Navy, son. But remember Fiona's saying."

Austin let his eyes land on the plaque on his wall, which Fiona had kept in her office.

Every single second
Of every single day

Every victim deserves my best

Next to it, he'd hung the plaque Anna had given him.

The world is worth fighting for.

"I know, mom. But the Navy is its own thing. It props up the whole economy around here, has its fingers in everything."

"Wait a minute. 'There's an *interesting* woman from NCIS named Symone Aoki.' I know that tone. That phrasing."

"*Mom*, please."

Run gave a whimper, then lay at his feet, her snout nosing around the tennis ball she'd tucked between her front legs.

"Don't 'mom' me. When you first had a crush on a girl back in high school, I remember you didn't come out and say it. You said, 'There's an *interesting* girl in the debate club who blah blah blah.' I *know* that tone. Just like your father. All formal and stuffy."

"Can we talk about—"

"Quiet, I'm Googling her."

Austin propped open the door and sat on the steps, tossing the ball across the yard. Now he'd done it. About a year after Fiona had died, his mom had begun hounding him for grandchildren. Every time he even mentioned a woman—could be a female co-worker, could be a lady who delivered his pizza—his mother swooned.

"Special Agent of the Major Case Response Team," his mother said slowly, probably reading from a website. "That's impressive. And, *ohhhhh*, she's gorgeous. You didn't tell me she was gorgeous."

"I didn't tell you anything, mom, other than the fact that she *exists*."

"Japanese heritage?" his mother asked.

"I don't know. I assume so. And yes, she's very pretty and—"

"Prettier than that reporter?"

"*Mom*, this isn't why I called." He'd told her about Anna only briefly and never mentioned her looks.

"I loved Fiona, too." His mother's tone had grown serious. "You know I did. She was the daughter I'd always wanted. I still cry for her. But you are young enough to have children. Fiona would want that. I know she would."

Austin watched the sun cut through the last of the mist, sparkling on the water. He knew his mother was right. Fiona would want him to move on. But knowing something was different from feeling it.

"You said Garrison mentioned I might be involved. Would *he* have asked for me to be part of this? I'm trying to figure out why the woman from NCIS approached me to begin with."

His mother was silent a while, as though deciding whether to let him wriggle out of the interrogation. "Captain Garrison is the only one there I knew who's at a high enough level. You never met him, I don't think, but he might know you're my son."

Austin considered this. "So he called you a few times, and you ignored it, then I got involved yesterday, and then you spoke with him last night?"

"Probably just a coincidence," his mom said.

Austin didn't reply, but he doubted it.

Run had been waiting patiently for his attention and he reached out and rubbed her head. His phone vibrated in his hand and he put the phone on speaker as his mom began a long diatribe about how he needed to have children and how cute his potential babies with Symone would be.

Ridley had sent him a text.

Got a letter from Sy demanding the return of all files related to the Memorial Day disappearance. Something very strange is going on here. Call me ASAP.

CHAPTER SEVEN

AUSTIN STARED at the message as his mother finished her monologue about her potential grandbabies. "You know, your father and I *loved* visiting Japan, too. If Symone *is* of Japanese descent, we could visit over there and, well, your father couldn't, but we'd work it all out."

"Mom, please." Austin instinctively kicked off his shoes at the entryway as Run shot passed him. They both went into the kitchen. "And before you say anything, *yes* I was listening and *no* I don't have any plans to have children. Not with the woman I met less than twenty-four hours ago, and not with anyone else." Before she could object, he added, "But you'll be the first person I call when that changes."

"Acceptable," she said. "One other thing. If you can help figure out what happened to those men, you have to do it. For me, for the Navy, for Fiona, and for yourself."

"I understand. Mom, I need to go. Tell dad I love him."

"I will."

They hung up and Austin poured himself a cup of coffee. Run sprawled out on the floor, blocking his path into the living room.

Austin stepped over her and called Ridley as he sat on the couch. "What's going on, Rid?"

"I'm sure you noticed Sy was acting strange yesterday, right?"

"I did."

"Well, after the call yesterday she went quiet, like she didn't want to share anything else with me, didn't even want to discuss the case. This morning we got a letter and... hold on..."

Austin heard footsteps and papers shuffling. "It's from the office of the NCIS Major Case Response Team. It says, 'To whom it may concern. We will no longer be communicating with the Kitsap Sheriff's Department concerning the case regarding the potential triple homicide at Foulweather Bluff. Please return any and all documents we have shared with you up to this point, and cease any and all investigations into this matter."

Austin kicked his feet up on the couch. "In other words, 'We'll take it from here.'"

Ridley chuckled. "More like, 'Go to hell. We'll take it from here.'"

"What are you thinking?" Austin asked.

"Could be a lot of things. But maybe they learned something, something they don't want out there."

"Maybe," Austin said. "Or maybe they just decided they want to keep it close. Could be a lot of things. Either way, I don't need any more convincing. They want us out, but I'm in."

"How soon can you be here?"

Austin stood and grabbed his jacket from a hook on the wall. "Just gotta ask Andy to take care of Run. Gimme an hour."

The drive took Austin past the Port Gamble S'Klallam reservation, through Poulsbo—a city known for its Viking-themed parade, views of the Olympics, and quaint, Norwegian vibes—and along an evergreen-lined stretch of highway into Silverdale. He'd lived in the area for a year and a half and thought he'd never get used to all the green. The land was green all year here, but in April and May, ferns and vines and blackberry bushes joined the chorus of evergreens, making the landscape even more lush.

He parked his truck at the Sheriff's department and hopped out. Despite his best efforts to ignore his mother's lecture, he had to admit that he was intrigued by Sy. He did find her beautiful, it was true, but there was something else. And it wasn't only that she had gone cagey about the case. She had a sadness to her that Austin knew well, the sadness of mourning that would never end, despite the fact that life went on. He wondered whether that's why she'd gone from cold to warm and back to cold so quickly. It didn't bother him, but it was confusing. It made him realize that his interactions with Anna might have come off in the exact same way.

At the end of the hallway, he found Ridley in the conference room, pacing in front of a giant whiteboard. To his surprise, Ridley's wife Rachel was sitting in the corner.

"Good to see you," Austin said.

She stood. "I was just leaving."

"Lucy and Jimmy are on their way," Ridley said.

Rachel wore a loose flowing dress and her dreadlocks were tied up in an elaborate bun.

"Congratulations on the baby," Austin said. "I've never seen Ridley in such a good mood."

She laughed. "Just gotta stay pregnant the rest of our lives together. That'll keep his blood pressure down."

Austin smiled. "How are you feeling?"

"Fine so far." She began walking out. "One of our cars is in the shop so I drove him in this morning."

"Well, good to see you," Austin said.

Ridley walked over and kissed Rachel goodbye, then watched her leave.

As happy as he was for Ridley, something in his heart twisted painfully. He'd learned to push it aside, but every time he saw a genuinely happy couple, it brought him back to what he'd had.

Jimmy and Lucy came in and sat as far away from each other as possible at the large folding table in the center of the room. They'd been on-again, off-again for years, Austin knew, and he could never tell what to expect when they walked in. His guess was that they were currently "on" since they'd arrived together, but had had some fight in the car on the way over.

Ridley tapped the pen on the whiteboard with a marker. "This morning I got a call from Sheriff Daniels."

"How is Mr. Nottingham?" Jimmy asked, taking a chug from a sugar-free energy drink.

Lucy offered a sarcastic frown. "Clever."

"This is serious," Ridley said. "He's at the Pacific Northwest Sheriff's Convention for the next three days, and, once I showed him the letter from NCIS, he gave me direct orders *not* to look into this case. We are not to take it a step further and I am not to allow any of my people to do so. I am *definitely* not supposed to procure the services of Thomas Austin, private investigator."

Lucy was twirling her finger nervously in her curly red hair.

Jimmy was popping his bicep muscles in his uniform. "Wait, so we're not going to try to solve this?"

"Of course we are," Ridley said, taping large photographs to the top of the whiteboard. "We just have to do it before he gets back to town."

He stepped out of the way, and Austin was staring at the young faces of the three Navy boys who'd disappeared thirty years ago, whose teeth had been found in the sand only yesterday.

The dread he'd felt when he'd first heard about the case had turned into an overwhelming sense of responsibility. It wasn't only that they'd been murdered. It wasn't only that they were Navy. Jack Hammeron, Joey Blake, and Adam Del Guado had been the best of the best, and they'd been murdered in uniform, while wearing medals attesting their valor.

This one mattered in a dozen ways Austin felt personally.

CHAPTER EIGHT

IN THE LITTLE meeting room of the Kitsap Sheriff's Department, Austin felt strangely at home. A year after moving to Washington State, Ridley had called him into the office to ask for help on an investigation. He'd been back a few times since wrapping up that first case, but as Ridley began scrawling out notes on the whiteboard, and as Jimmy and Lucy gave off some odd vibes Austin was unable to read, he realized he was exactly where he was meant to be.

He believed Fiona's credo—every victim *did* deserve his best —but it was more than that. Austin loved this work. And, he realized for the first time since he'd left the NYPD, he genuinely missed it.

"So," Ridley said, "Symone and her team have the bones, the bullets, the crime scene, the man and woman power, and a helluva lot more time, money and resources than we do."

Jimmy laughed. "And we've got?"

"Shoeleather," Ridley said. "And local connections."

"I don't know," Lucy said. "I hear the Navy is kinda big around here. They may have a connection or two as well."

Ridley sighed. "So just the shoe leather, then." He pointed at the pictures. "This is what it's all about."

Joey Blake had been the youngest of the three—twenty-four when they disappeared—but in the picture he looked like a teenager. Pale white skin and a buzzcut that made his face look round as a baby's. Jack Hammeron was darker skinned—maybe biracial, Austin thought—with curly black hair and a square jaw that made him look like a GI Joe. Adam Del Guado was leaner than the others, his face bony and scarred from acne or perhaps chicken pox.

Austin stood and walked a lap around the table. "Here's what I don't understand." He looked to Jimmy, then Lucy. "And I don't know how much Rid filled you in, but twenty-four hours ago, Sy wanted Ridley's help. And my help. Well, she didn't *want* it, but someone made her ask for it. Then, suddenly, she blocks us out like we're enemies. I don't see how that happens unless she or someone above her knows what happens and doesn't want it solved."

He sat back down.

Everyone was silent.

Austin had considered easing into his theory, but Ridley's warning that Sheriff Daniels would be back in three days had lit a fire under him.

"Not gonna lie," Lucy said, "I had the same thought. But I'm glad I'm not the one who casually threw out the notion that NCIS could be involved in a massive cover up."

"It's too soon to go there," Ridley said.

"I know," Austin said. "It's just... I don't see how else this ends. Sometimes when one faction tries to pull back a case it's just territorial bickering, but sometimes it's a lot worse."

Jimmy held up his phone. "Mark Davidovich. From my read of the files, the first investigation focused on him fairly quickly. Former business partner of one of the deceased, right?"

Austin nodded. He'd read that part of the file.

"That's right," Ridley said. "Jack Hammeron. Hammer, they called him. He and Davidovich were trying to start a sports bar or something. Had a falling out. Austin, what did you see? Nothing there, right?"

Austin nodded. To him it had looked like a classic case of the investigators locking in on a suspect way too soon, letting a hundred other threads go unexamined. And when it turned out Davidovich was in the clear—he'd been in another state at the time of the disappearance—investigators were left with nothing. "Worth doubling back, but yeah, shoddy work by the original team. Davidovich had financial motive, but they were arguing over ten grand or something. I don't see how that leads him to take out all three men. Or how he even could have gotten them all there to begin with."

Samantha walked in, holding a laptop under each arm. Her warm, smiling face was always a welcome sight, and not only because Austin needed her help on the issue of the laptop he'd been told to get.

In the last month, Samantha had finished her degree and been promoted from intern to full-time tech specialist. She'd gotten a new tattoo to commemorate the occasion, apparently. On her forearm, she now had a small black graduation cap tattooed next to the Chinese calligraphy weaving its way up her forearm.

"So," Jimmy said as she sat at the table next to him. "Now that you're full time, you're doubling up on laptops?"

"Some of us can do two things at once," she snapped back playfully.

Lucy offered a high-five that Samantha met squarely. "Good job, Sam-Bam. Part of working here full time is insulting Jimmy whenever possible. Your holiday bonus is dependent on it."

Jimmy feigned a hurt expression. "Lucy O'Let-Me-Down."

Samantha chuckled. "Is having a lame nickname part of the job as well?"

Austin smiled. "Indeed it is, Sam-Bam."

Ridley crossed his arms. "We done?"

Everyone sat up a little straighter.

"Like I said," Ridley continued, "Daniels is back in three days and this investigation is one hundred percent off the record. Well, off the record from him, at least."

Everyone nodded.

Ridley leaned on the wall. "Samantha, what have you got?"

She tapped one of the laptops and addressed the group. "Ridley asked me to look into publicly available information on the case, both before and after the medals were found. Now, it's *possible* NCIS has people running AI searches as good as me, but I doubt it. What I found was interesting. Besides a few decent rumors, like the three deceased getting into a big argument at the Watering Hole the night they disappeared, there's not much good information out there. There is, however, *a lot* of information."

She plugged one of the laptops into a projector in the center of the table, which cast her screen onto the blank wall next to the whiteboard. A graph popped up and the wall became covered in dotted blue lines. "The blue lines represent the amount of chatter about the case. See how they go up over time?"

Austin nodded. "Isn't that just more people coming online?"

"Exactly," Samantha said. "When the case started in ninety-two, basically no one was online. So, as there were more and more message boards about true crime, famous cold cases, and so on, chatter increased."

"So what's the big deal?" Jimmy asked.

She clicked her keyboard and the image on the wall changed. "This graph shows the expected amount of online chatter relative to the reports in major news outlets. The more the big networks and newspapers cover something, the more mentions you see on blogs, on Twitter and Facebook, right?"

Austin crossed and uncrossed his legs. He was growing impatient.

Samantha clicked again. "This red line is the actual amount of online commentary relative to the number of major media stories."

Austin studied it. The red line was nearly off the top of the graph. He could tell what she was trying to say, but not what it meant.

Samantha said, "You're looking at me like I'm trying to explain an iPhone to a caveman. Lemme put it this way: since the discovery of the medals and the bones, there have been no major media stories about this case. CNN isn't on it, Fox isn't, the *Seattle Times* hasn't even popped across the water. That's because it hasn't leaked."

Austin nodded. "Anna Downey is pretty plugged in and she told me she can't get anything. She was nibbling around the edges."

Samantha snapped. "Exactly. And yet..." she drew her finger across the red line on the wall. "And yet millions of *people* are talking about it online. Throwing out ideas, rumors, theories. So many accounts are talking about it, some newspapers are now covering the online commentary because they still can't get a real scoop."

Ridley cleared his throat. "So what does that mean?"

"Disinformation," Lucy said.

"Lucy O'Right-You-Are," Samantha said. "A firehose of disinformation has been sprayed at the Internet."

"By whom?" Austin asked.

Samantha shut her laptop. "Tens of thousands of accounts."

Ridley paced. "So someone who knew about the medals and bones wanted to get out ahead of this thing and spread all sorts of theories, just to muddle everything up?"

"That's what I'm thinking," Samantha said.

"It's a Russian specialty," Jimmy said, "that brand of disin-formation."

Austin looked at Jimmy. "There was a rare Russian bullet at the scene."

Samantha opened her computer again, bringing up an image of a similar bullet on the wall. "Ridley mentioned it earlier, and I confirmed. Although tons of Russian surplus ammo flooded the U.S. markets in the nineties, this type of pistol and ammo was experimental. Very little of it exists."

"It's not nothing," Austin said, "but it ain't much."

"So here's the plan," Ridley said. "Austin and Lucy, you go see Maria Del Guado. She's the widow of Adam Del Guado, still living in Bremerton. She was twenty-six at the time, now fifty-six and remarried to a guy named Percy... something."

"Perry Diaz, age fifty-eight," Samantha said, sliding a file to Austin. "He has a sheet. Two arrests. Just bar fight stuff. No convictions."

Austin took the file. "So what will you and Jimmy do?"

Ridley smiled. "Sy thinks she can box us out, but I have a friend in the Navy."

"Her boss?" Austin asked.

"Nah, someone high up, but not directly over her. Just gonna feel her out, see if she might know what's going on."

"Ask her about Captain Garrison," Austin said.

Ridley frowned. "He's high up and I'm not asking anything about him that could get her in trouble."

Austin said, "He used to know my mom. Had a thing for her, apparently. I think he's the one who asked Sy to involve me."

Ridley seemed skeptical. "Doubt I can find out anything on that, but I'll try." He surveyed the room. "So we have a plan?"

Everyone nodded.

"Looks like it's you and me again, New York," Lucy said. "Like old times."

Austin smiled. "I'll meet you at your car."

On the way out, Austin pulled Samantha aside and explained the task he wanted help with, then offered her a couple hundred bucks to help him find the right laptop and set it up. He needed to make sure he got this right.

She gave him a mildly condescending smile. "You want help going to Best Buy, purchasing a laptop, and installing a free app?"

Austin smiled back, half embarrassed, half annoyed. "I know I'm about a hundred years old. But this is the most important thing I'll ever..." He couldn't let himself finish the sentence. "This is very important to me. I don't trust myself not to screw it up. Tomorrow morning?"

Samantha nodded. "They open at ten. We can go from here."

CHAPTER NINE

"TELL ME ABOUT THE BULLET," Lucy said, easing out of the parking lot.

"Beyond rare," Austin said, cracking the window and letting the cool breeze fill the car. The air smelled of sweet grass and salty beach, with a thickness that filled his lungs. "Do you ever get used to how nice the air is here?"

"I'm used to it. But a friend who visited from New York told me once that it's the reward we earn for six months of gray drizzle."

"Worth it," Austin said. "Back to the bullet. What's more interesting than that is the gun it was designed to be used in." He opened his email, where he'd sent himself a photo of it. "Gerasimenko VAG-72 or VAG-73. Dual compartment magazine with 48-round capacity. Projectile is all-steel, except for a screw-in base made of brass, and it's hollow at the rear, where the propellant is stored. Very, very rare firearm." He set his phone on his lap. "It's the kind of thing only collectors have nowadays. Even back in the nineties, they were almost impossible to find. Exactly the kind of thing you do not want to use in a murder, assuming you don't want to get caught."

"Unless you're trying to send a message of some sort."

"True, but when you're trying to send a message, you don't bury the body in a marshland on an isolated, protected beach where no one will ever find it." He thought for a moment. "If there was any Russian connection here, they'd either have committed the murders with regular weapons and stashed the bodies, or used the rare gun but made sure people found out about it. It's the combination that doesn't add up."

"Good point, which makes me think this was a crime of passion. Maybe a collector had the gun and used it unplanned?"

"Not a bad angle," Austin said. He tapped out a quick email to Samantha, asking her to dig around and find out if she could get anything on gun collectors in the area, especially ones with an interest in rare Russian firearms. "I asked Samantha to do her Internet magic."

"Whoever thought we'd be able to solve cases from time to time just from things idiots put on the internet, accidentally incriminating themselves."

Austin laughed. "Although I guess modern detective work requires having people who know how to find it. It's not like she's running a simple Google search."

"Okay," Lucy said, weaving around a line of trucks that had been blocking traffic, "that's the gun, at least one of them, but assuming the speculation at the scene was right, why kill one man with a rare Russian collectible and the others with a standard rifle. Two shooters?"

"Possible, but..." It didn't add up. In crimes with multiple gunmen, things were usually coordinated, planned. He couldn't think of any situation where the plan would be to use a rare and very traceable pistol alongside a regular rifle. "You pull anything else out of the files?"

Lucy frowned. "Jimmy was stuck on the argument angle. Two different witnesses said the three men had been arguing outside the Watering Hole the night they disappeared."

"From the initial report, there was nothing indicating why."

"But there was something else," Lucy said. "A third witness said that Adam Del Guado was arguing with someone. *One* other person."

Austin hadn't seen that. "Could be confused, or maybe that witness didn't see the whole thing."

She squeezed the wheel, clearly frustrated. "The file was total crap. Unclear whether the witnesses were all talking about the same argument, or what. It's possible there were two arguments. Maybe the three deceased were arguing about sports or something, and maybe Adam Del Guado had a separate argument with someone else."

"Worth pursuing with Del Guado's wife."

Austin had noticed a new ring on Lucy's freckled ring finger when she took out her frustration on the steering wheel. A simple diamond set in a gold band. Austin had come to trust his gut when it came to most things, but he was curious whether his sense that something was different between Lucy and Jimmy was right. He was far from a ring expert, but... "Is that an *engagement* ring?"

Lucy flinched slightly. "It is."

"Uhh, I don't want to pry, but..."

"I'm engaged." She opened her mouth as though she was going to say more, then shot Austin an odd look and said nothing.

Now Austin was confused. Had she gotten engaged to someone else? That would explain the iciness between her and Jimmy. "I'm getting the sense that you don't want to talk about it."

"It's kinda your fault."

"*My* fault?" Now Austin was *very* confused.

Lucy scrunched up her nose, but said nothing.

He stared at her, eyebrow raised, as she got off the freeway and executed a series of evasive maneuvers, taking them into one of the more rundown neighborhoods in Bremerton. She seemed to be choosing her next words so carefully that she chose to remain silent.

Finally, she said, "*You're* the one who convinced me to go for him."

"So it *is* Jimmy?"

She shot him a look and, for the first time, he could see the happiness in her face. But it was an odd happiness, like she was trying to conceal it to be professional, or perhaps that she couldn't even believe it herself.

"We haven't told anyone yet," she said.

"Why not?"

"I think we're both in shock."

Austin laughed. "This is one of the oddest reactions to an engagement I've ever seen."

"Not exactly Instagram-ready, is it?"

"I guess not," Austin said.

"It's hard to explain. Both of our parents got divorced. We haven't seen a lot of successful marriages. I don't know... I thought it would feel *different*. I don't know what I thought."

Ahead of them, multiple TV vans were parked in front of a single-story house with a chain-link fence enclosing a small patch of grass. Apparently, word had gotten out about the case, which had led reporters to Maria Del Guado's house.

Austin pointed at the small crowd that had gathered on the outside of the fence. "I want to hear more about this, but for now, we should focus on the fact that this story is about to blow up."

Maria Del Guado's living room was small, and full of ducks.

Ducks wearing diapers.

Austin had begun feeling a sense of unreality during Lucy's

bizarre admission that she was engaged, but now he felt as though he'd entered the Twilight Zone.

He sat next to Lucy on a dirty couch, staring at a giant cross on the wall, which hung over a fireplace. Around his feet, six or seven ducks waddled back and forth, all wearing customized cloth diapers printed with colorful plaid patterns, or tiny flowers, animals, or stars.

On the opposite side of the living room, a strapping young man who'd introduced himself as "Hammer Junior" sat, staring daggers at them. He looked to be in his early thirties and was the spitting image of his dad: same square jaw, same curly black hair, same awesome size.

Maria and her husband Perry returned from the kitchen. She carried a tray of red Kool Aid and glasses; he carried a pack of napkins.

"Can we make this quick?" Maria asked, setting the tray of drinks on the coffee table and sitting cross-legged on the floor, taking one of the ducks into her lap. "I just sold my story to Inside Edition for twenty-five thousand dollars, and I don't have a lot of time to repeat myself to the lousy officers who failed to solve my husband's murder for the last thirty years."

Austin sat in stunned silence, looking from Maria to her husband, then to Hammer Junior. He almost said something sarcastic like, "Thanks for the warm welcome," but thought better of it, deciding to let Lucy lead the charge.

The remaining ducks had gathered around her on the floor, mostly quiet but offering up occasional quacks and flaps.

"Help yourself to some red drink," she said, offering up an overly-sweet smile as she pulled a handful of grain out of her pocket and began feeding it to the ducks.

CHAPTER TEN

LUCY'S FACE had reddened at Maria's mention of selling her story to Inside Edition. "Mrs. Del Guado—"

"Maria, please call me Maria. I called Adam 'Addie.' He hated it, but I didn't care. I say when you sign a marriage license it gives you license to call them whatever you want." She tossed a little pile of grain on the carpet and the ducks went to work pecking at it.

"It's true," her husband said. "She calls me Purr, like a cat. Always has. Even though my name is *Perry*, like the fruit."

Lucy said, "I appreciate that the offer of money to sell your story is tempting, but—"

"This is America," Maria said, "I can sell my story if I want."

Lucy folded her arms and stared her down. "And you can also speak with the police, whether or not you want." Softening, she said, "Maria, we know you've been through this before, but we have new information and we only want to get to the bottom of this. Now, how long have you and Perry been married?"

Austin recognized this tactic. Lucy already knew the answer because it had been in the file. But she wanted to see how they'd respond, what it might bring to the surface.

"Twenty-odd years," Perry said.

"Twenty-nine years," Maria corrected. "And I *know*, it was weird to get married again only a year after Addie disappeared. And no, we weren't having any marital issues when he disappeared. But we married young. We were better friends than romantic partners. Honestly think he might have been gay, but it wasn't a time when you could admit that in the Navy."

As Lucy jotted notes, Austin was watching Hammer Junior out of the corner of his eye. He was roughly the size of Ridley, well over six feet with the shoulders and chest of an NFL linebacker. "Do you have any memories of your father?" Austin asked.

"I was three when he died. No." His voice was hard as iron, but Austin didn't think it was personal. Hammer Junior came across as a guy who'd had a tough life and was generally pissed at the world, not at anyone in particular.

"What about your mother?" Austin asked. "Her name was Maria as well, I believe."

"Died a few years back," Hammer Junior said. "We moved to the east coast in ninety-six, and I came back here as soon as I could. Joined the Navy at eighteen. Been all over, but Maria and Perry here were like the mom and dad I never had. My mom's a drunk."

Austin studied him. It wasn't unheard of to hear a son talk about his deceased mom that way, but it was odd, to be sure. He was clearly bitter.

Lucy glanced up. "Maria, we've been reviewing the old files and there are multiple reports of arguments that occurred in the bar in Hansville the night your husband went missing."

"Like I told the lady from NCIS, like I told all you people at the time, those three guys were close as brothers, no way anything got between them."

One of the ducks waddled over to the corner and let itself out an oversized doggie door into a little side yard. As strange as this was, it didn't crack Austin's top five for oddest encounters during an interview. After all, he'd worked in New York City for two decades.

"I understand," Lucy said. "But there was another report. That perhaps Addie had argued with someone else that evening, not his friends, but another party entirely. Male, brown hair was the only description. The file is, well, a little unclear."

Austin allowed his eyes to fall on Perry, who was maybe five foot ten with light brown hair. When Perry met his eyes, Austin tilted his head slightly, asking the question without asking it.

"I never even met Adam," Perry said. "And I have nothing but love for his memory." He waved at the cross on the wall, as though that might somehow prove his case.

"What line of work are you in?" Austin asked him.

"We own a couple gyms," Perry said, "smoothie bar and a vitamin shop attached to one of them."

Lucy took a few notes.

Austin tried to ignore the duck examining his shoe. "All three men were in uniform that night. Why was that?"

Maria sighed. "Memorial Day service for a friend."

Austin already knew this as well. "Did they hang out at the Watering Hole often?"

"No," Maria said. "That was one of the weird things. I mean I guess it makes sense that they were drinking there because they were in Hansville for the Memorial Day service, but... at the time we lived right down the street from Ace's. That's where Addie and I used to hang. To be honest, I was a little pissed that he chose to hang out with his buddies instead of coming back home."

Austin crossed his leg to keep the duck from pecking at his shoe, but the duck just moved to the other foot.

This was going nowhere, and Austin could sense Lucy's frustration.

"Maria," she said. "Is there anything else you can tell us,

anything you haven't already told the police, told CSI, told Inside Edition?"

"I haven't told Inside Edition the big one yet."

Austin and Lucy perked up simultaneously.

"The big what?" Lucy asked.

Maria leaned forward and poured herself a glass of Kool Aid, which had been ignored up until this point. She took a long sip, savoring the moment. "Now, at the time I didn't know anything about this, but..." she trailed off, glancing at Hammer Junior, then at Perry.

Perry nodded. "They *did* say to start the hype train."

"What are you talking about?" Austin asked.

Perry scratched the hair of his short beard. "The folks at Inside Edition, we promised them something big. Not solve-the-case big. That's not what the show is about. But something new, something that hasn't come out yet. They said the show would get more viewers if the revelation started kinda seeping into the ether beforehand."

"Don't tell them," Hammer Junior said, his voice as hard as his name.

"Lemme put it this way," Maria said. "I promise if I knew everything I would tell you, but have you heard of Admiral Tom Vellory?"

"Admiral TV?" Lucy asked. "I think I voted for him in the presidential primary in 2012, or was that 2008? Anyway, of course we've heard of him."

Austin knew the name—and the persona—well. Vellory was a two-star Admiral who'd retired in 2006, written a few books, and performed well on the lecture circuit. In 2008 he'd thrown his hat in the ring in the presidential primary, running as a moderate, pro-military candidate. He'd lost, but it had elevated his stature and sold a lot more books. Ever since, he'd been a regular on TV, staying out of political commentary but becoming one of the most trusted names when it came to the ways of war. Austin had read once that he'd appeared on TV so much, even his wife had started calling him Admiral TV.

In the nineties, he commanded a Naval vessel that had been involved in the Persian Gulf War. All three of the deceased men had served under him, and he'd been at the memorial in Hansville the day his men had gone missing, as well as at the Watering Hole later that night.

"What about him?" Austin asked.

Maria held up both of her hands, as though professing her innocence. "I'm not saying... I'm just saying."

Lucy folded her arms. "I'm not sure if it's the duck crap or you, Mrs. Del Guado, but I'm starting to get pissed off. If you have any information that is relevant, tell me now or tell me later today at the station, after I haul you down there in front of all the cameras. And I'll make sure to keep you there until you miss your interview."

Perry smirked. "That might add buzz to the show. *Interview Postponed as Police Try to Silence Widow. Tonight at Ten on Inside Edition.*"

Lucy stood abruptly, causing a group of ducks to scurry away quacking. "What about Admiral Vellory?"

Maria leaned in conspiratorially. "Everyone thinks he's so great. Maybe he ain't. I'm not saying nothin' more."

Hammer Junior cleared his throat. "This is ridiculous. Maria, I'm sorry, but this is..." his temples popped like his head might explode, then he let out a long breath. "Before she died, my mom told me that Admiral Vellory might have been involved in something shady while in Operation Desert Storm. I believe it was him who my dad and the others were arguing with that night."

Lucy took some notes, then looked up. "Any idea what shady things he may have been involved in?"

Hammer Junior shook his head. "No, and look, I respect the

man. I'm Navy through and through. But if he is in any way involved in my dad's death, I'll kill him myself."

"Wait wait wait," Lucy said. "You don't just throw that out there."

"It's true," Maria said.

"What's true?" Austin asked.

"Me and the other Maria—Hammer's widow—used to talk about it. It didn't seem like anything, but we both thought our husbands might have been up to something when they were over in the Gulf. Something involving Vellory. I was never gonna say nothing about it, but when Hammer Junior brought it up..."

"Something shady like what?" Austin asked.

Maria folded her arms. Perry took the tray of Kool Aid back to the kitchen. Hammer Junior stood and opened the door.

A photographer leaned across the fence and snapped pictures of them inside the living room.

"I'm not saying," Maria said. "I'm just saying."

CHAPTER ELEVEN

ADMIRAL TOM "TV" Vellory lived in a large but modest-looking house overlooking the bay in Poulsbo. At least four-thousand square feet, it could only be reached down a long dirt road, which Lucy had navigated with a white-knuckled grip on the steering wheel.

Austin had been surprised when Vellory agreed to meet with them only a few hours after their visit to the duck-filled home of Maria Del Guado, but Lucy had been worried. Vellory had been famous since she could remember. She hadn't only voted for him in the 2008 primary. Upon questioning, she'd admitted to donating twenty bucks to his campaign and having a poster of him on her wall. As she put it, "Some girls grew up idolizing the Backstreet Boys or whatever band was hot, I grew up idolizing men who promised a compassionate domestic policy and a strong foreign policy."

Austin laughed. "I guess there are worse qualities to admire in someone."

She turned off the car and they stared up at the house from the stone parking area out front.

"I still don't get why he agreed to this," Lucy said.

"Don't worry," Austin said. "Not everything is bad news. He may actually want to help get to the bottom of this. And you'll get to meet someone you admire. It's a win-win."

"It's just... Getting to his level in the Navy is half valor, half politics, from what I hear. We really don't want to screw up in there. He's probably one of the five most powerful people in the state."

"He's retired, and not exactly young anymore. You sure it isn't that you're starstruck?"

She frowned. "Can't it be both?"

"We won't mess up," Austin said, leading the way up the steps and ringing the doorbell. "If you get nervous, I'll take the lead."

As the echo of the doorbell died down, a woman in an old fashioned black and white maid outfit opened the door. Austin had never seen one of those outfits outside a movie.

The maid inspected them. She was in her fifties, with a neat blond ponytail and a disapproving look on her face. "Ms. O'Rourke and Mr. Austin?"

They both nodded.

"Mr. Vellory is expecting you."

Although the house looked modest from the outside, the inside was as nice as the lakefront mansion in Seattle in which, a couple months back, Austin had spent more time than he cared to remember. Everything looked either brand new or vintage and recently polished. Though Austin didn't know much about furnishings or moldings, everything screamed class, charm, and wealth. In fact, everything was so nice that Austin wondered whether Vellory left the outside of his house modest-looking on purpose. He could clearly afford to upgrade it to match the inside.

The maid led them to a second floor study, where Vellory was sitting in a giant leather chair, reading a magazine. He stood as they entered, removing his reading glasses and running a hand through his full head of silver-white hair. "Hell of a thing." He shook his head. "Thanks for coming."

Vellory was in his seventies, like Austin's dad, but looked twenty years younger. His skin was taut, like stretched leather, and his rigid posture reminded Austin of his mom's admonitions to "sit up straight." After a few minutes of small talk, which included praise of the home and Lucy gushing about his first book, Vellory changed the subject back to the discovery at Foulweather Bluff.

"I've heard some things." He shook his head sadly. "As glad as I am that perhaps those boys might get some justice, there was part of me that wanted to believe they were still out there somewhere, alive. Of course, I'm not that naive, but, you know, part of you simply clings to that hope."

"I appreciate you meeting us," Lucy said. "May I ask why you did?"

Vellory smiled warmly. "Why I agreed to meet? Three of my men disappeared. It appears they were murdered, though I'm still coming to terms with that. Just because it was thirty years ago doesn't mean they aren't still my men."

His speech was practiced and warm, though he didn't come off as insincere. His tone was somewhere between a wise grandfather and battle-hardened soldier. He'd seen it all, done it all, and could hold his own in any fight, in any meeting room, but he might also bounce a grandkid on his knee or tell dad jokes on the back nine of the local golf course. There was a reason he was good on TV.

He walked to the large window that looked out across a bright-green lawn, which led down to the water. Two boats were tied to an old wooden dock. "I'll tell you, those men were three of the best. Kills me that they made it through some of the toughest fighting in Iraq only to lose their lives back home."

"You were one of the last to see them alive," Lucy offered, "according to the file."

"As far as I know that's right."

"Do you mind walking us through it?" she asked.

"Not at all." He returned to the overstuffed leather chair and crossed his right leg over his left. "We'd been at the Hansville cemetery to honor a fellow serviceman. One of our boys who didn't make it out. Afterwards, we headed down to the Watering Hole for a beer and to watch the Mariner's game. One thing led to another, and it was Memorial Day, so we weren't buying. Old Bakes let us drink for free. No one was getting drunk, mind you, just slowly sipping and enjoying the day. It was like today, sunny, but cooler. When you've seen battle like I have —like those three men had—you learn to enjoy the little things."

He paused, and Austin noticed that he'd been hanging on Vellory's every word. One of the cardinal sins of a detective was to be in awe of a witness or a suspect. It clouded the mind and caused investigators to miss important details. He focused in, trying to take in the words without being sedated by Vellory's warm, hypnotic voice.

Vellory had mentioned Bakes, the man who'd sold Austin his store. He'd been interviewed in the initial investigation as well, but, like much of the case file, his interview was thin and not especially helpful.

Lucy said, "How many drinks would you say everyone had?"

"I had two," Vellory said. "Exactly two. I made a rule for myself when I was young. Never more than two drinks in a day, and I've not broken it once. Saw enough men get taken down by the affliction of alcohol." He shook his head sadly. "The others... well, maybe three or four beers each, but that was over as many hours."

"And you left at what time?" Austin asked.

Vellory considered this. "Around eight."

"And all three of your men were still there?" Lucy asked.

Vellory nodded. "I told the boys, just like I did when they

were under my command. I told them, 'Be bad, but in a good way.'" He smiled fondly. "Little saying we had back then."

Austin cocked his head, but Lucy asked the question before he had the chance. "And what did it mean?"

The maid returned and offered them coffee or soft drinks. They all declined and Vellory waved her away.

"When you're in a fight," he said as the door closed, "you know what you're doing is bad. It never feels good to kill another man. Only way we can do our job, do what needs to be done, is to know that we're being bad for a greater good. So we say, 'Be bad, but in a good way.' I wanted the baddest men I could find, but ones with honor, with morals, with a higher purpose. In Adam, Hammer, and Joey, I had them." He dropped his face and Austin saw real emotion in his pale blue eyes.

"In the files," Lucy said. "There's mention of an argument between the three of them."

"Those three argued all the time," Vellory said, looking up. "Like brothers."

"What were they arguing about that night?" Austin asked.

Vellory shrugged. "Sports, women, who knows. I remember Hammer always ribbing Adam about his wife. Hammer's wife was a real looker. Adam's wife, well... Anyway, they were both named Maria, you know. And Hammer would always say things like, Ugly Maria and Hot Maria."

"Sounds mean," Lucy said.

"First of all, it was the nineties. Back then you could make a joke and not get dragged over the coals for it. Second, those men had fought together, stood over dead friends together. Any joking they did was in fun."

The maid returned briefly and said, "Twenty minutes, sir," then left without explanation.

Vellory glanced at his watch. "I have a CNN segment coming up. Embarrassed to say it, but I need to get to the makeup chair. Part of the job."

Lucy asked, "So you don't think there's any chance there was a real argument between them?"

He sat up even straighter, as though preparing to stand. "Nothing that would have to do with their death."

"That evening," Austin said. "Did you see Adam Del Guado arguing with *another* man? There is some confusion in the files about it."

Vellory thought for a moment, then shook his head slowly. "I remember it being a great night, full of positivity, stories, and typical BS."

"Did Del Guado leave the bar for any period of time?"

"Not that I recall. I'm sure he used the bathroom at some point, and I guess it's possible he went outside and had a run-in. But nothing I saw."

"Was he a smoker?" Austin asked.

"He was."

"So it's possible he may have popped outside for a smoke, gotten in an argument with someone, and you wouldn't have seen it?"

"Possible." Vellory stood. "I really have to go."

He approached Austin and shook his hand warmly, then leaned in and gave Lucy a brief hug. She blushed, then stepped back.

"If there's anything I can do to help as you work this case," Vellory said as he ushered them toward the door, "please don't hesitate to ask."

Back in the car, Austin and Lucy looked up at the house through the windshield. "He hugged me," Lucy said. "If I'd told an eighteen-year-old me that one day I'd be asking Tom Vellory questions about a triple homicide, and that he'd hug me, I'd..."

Austin pulled out his phone. "Have called me crazy?"

"Crazier than crazy."

"He seems like a good guy, just like he comes across on TV," Austin said. "But there's something I don't get."

Lucy started the car. "What's that?"

Austin scrolled through the files Ridley had sent to him, the ones they were supposed to have returned. There were dozens of different attachments to the email, but he found the one he was looking for as Lucy made it to the end of the driveway.

"I *did* have it right," Austin said, pleased with himself.

"What?"

"What time did Vellory say he left the Watering Hole that night?"

"Eight o'clock," Lucy said.

Austin held up his phone, but Lucy kept her eyes on the road.

"Back in ninety-two," Austin said, "he told investigators he left a little before ten o'clock."

Lucy considered this. "Could be a simple misremembering. Or an error in the file."

"Could be, but here, lemme read from the file. 'Vellory stated that he left about twenty minutes before ten o'clock and reached home a few minutes after ten, where he watched the ten o'clock news.'" Austin shoved his phone back in his pocket. "That's pretty specific to be an error in the file."

"So he misremembered." She glanced over, her face scrunched in skepticism. "It's been thirty years, New York. I can barely remember what time I got home yesterday."

Vellory struck Austin as the kind of guy who rarely misremembered, and never misspoke. "Does he seem like the kind of guy who does a lot of misremembering?"

"No, but..."

"It's only five o'clock, and I know a guy who might be able to clear this up."

"I was supposed to meet Jimmy."

"Wedding planning?"

She looked surprised. "Hell no. It takes us half an hour to plan where to go for dinner. We're a *looooooooong* way from wedding plans."

"So the engagement is..."

"More of a placeholder. A reminder that, at some point in the not-too-distant future, we should consider possibly making wedding plans. The engagement ring is like a tiny bullet point at the bottom of our to-do list."

Austin laughed. "So it sounds like you could delay your meetup an hour or two."

"Okay, but why?"

Austin tapped the location of Buck Lake into her dashboard GPS. "Have you ever been lake fishing?"

CHAPTER TWELVE

WHEN AUSTIN HAD PURCHASED his store and apartment, he'd never once spoken with the previous owner. The man's name was Butch Baker, and he was a local legend everyone called "Bakes."

His grandfather and father had both been Puget Sound fishermen, but Bakes had disappointed both of them and gone to culinary school, then scraped together every penny he could to open the Watering Hole in 1986. At the time, Hansville was even more sparsely populated, so he'd struggled to attract customers. But he'd made the place work and had managed it himself for thirty-five years before selling it to Austin. Word around town was that he'd never married and never had children because he only loved the Watering Hole.

Austin had tried to get in touch with him during the negotiations, but Bakes had wanted to do everything through their real estate agents, and that's how the deal had gone down.

The odd thing was, he lived only a quarter mile from the store and, as far as Austin knew, he hadn't stepped foot inside once in the year and a half Austin had owned it.

As a general rule, Austin didn't take things personally unless he had a good reason to. He'd figured Bakes had his reasons for doing things the way he did, and he'd never thought much of it. So the only thing he knew about Bakes' current life was that he fished at every possible moment, sometimes from the various shores on the Puget Sound, but often at Buck Lake, a small, trout-stocked lake only about a mile from his store.

On a gorgeous evening in May, just as the sun was beginning to set, Austin was sure they'd find him there.

As they got out of the car, Austin pointed across the lake, where a man was casting his line from a small area of treeless waterfront. "Like I thought."

"How should we approach it?" Lucy asked.

"Don't know a lot about his personality, so let's just wing it."

The shore was densely forested, so they took a trail that wound a quarter mile through the trees before coming out at a little patch of well-trodden bank that appeared to be a favorite spot for local anglers. The section of lake was mostly free of reeds and lily pads.

"Mr. Baker," Austin called from a few yards away.

Bakes had his foot wedged against a root that jutted out of the ground at an angle. He turned slowly, leaving his line in the water.

"Who's asking?" Bakes was around seventy, with a round face and Santa Claus beard that made him look much more jolly than his tone implied. He eyed them for a moment, frowned, then turned back to the lake and began reeling in his line.

Lucy stepped forward. "Lucy O'Rourke, Kitsap Sheriff's office. This is Thomas Austin."

When his line was in, he tucked the pole under his arm and turned. "Not often someone interrupts trout time. Better have a good reason."

As far as Austin could tell, Bakes didn't even recognize his name. He extended a hand. "Bakes—can I call you Bakes?—I'm Thomas Austin. You sold me your store."

Bakes scratched at his beard. "New York?"

"I'll answer to that," Austin said, trying to sound friendly. "I tried to get in touch with you. Multiple times."

Bakes looked from Austin to Lucy. "You here to arrest me because I didn't want to talk to you?"

Austin laughed. "No, another matter. But, out of curiosity, why didn't you?"

Bakes huffed, turned to the lake, and took his pole in his hand like he might cast it, then rested it on his shoulder and turned back. "Everyone was pissed at me for selling to a foreigner. I couldn't face it."

Austin almost laughed, but it was clear Bakes wasn't joking. "New York is in America, Bakes. Not to mention, I lived in Bremerton for a while when I was a kid. And San Diego, and Connecticut, and—"

"You're a New Yorker. Everyone wanted me to sell it to Sheriff Daniels, or the Johnson boys over in Kingston." He stroked his beard. "I took the highest offer."

"Well," Austin said, "I appreciate that, and I hope I've done the place justice."

"Heard you tore up my kitchen." His tone was accusatory, but not exactly angry. That tiny kitchen and the bar it served had been his baby, his home for decades. Of course, Austin had known this when he planned the renovation, but the place had needed it. Badly.

"We updated a little, yes."

"Heard your food is better than mine," Bakes said. He frowned, then slowly extended his hand for Austin to shake.

Austin took his hand, which was thick and calloused. "I'm sure people are just telling you that to rib you. From what I hear, your year-round Thanksgiving dinner was something to write home about."

Lucy cleared her throat. "As much as I'm enjoying this walk down bromance lane, we have something serious to talk about."

Bakes ignored her and smiled at Austin. "Damn right it was. The key is in the gravy. If your gravy is good enough, you can slop in on an old tennis shoe and people will think you're Julia Child." He assessed Austin for a moment, then nodded approvingly and turned back to the lake, tossing his line deftly about forty yards before beginning to reel it back in slowly. "Ask away, Ms. O'Rourke."

"You heard about the discovery at Foulweather Bluff?" she asked.

"Sure I did. Terrible thing, but no surprise. I stopped hoping for those boys to return a long time ago. Three soldiers don't just go missing and it turns out they're fine."

"We've already read all your statements," Lucy said, "the ones you made at the time of the disappearance and the ones you made when the case was reopened. We're wondering if anything about the discovery of the medals, the bones... well, we're wondering if any of it brought up memories you might have forgotten."

"Can't say it did, but I admit I haven't heard much. You say you found their bones?"

Austin grimaced. "All three men. It's been confirmed."

Bakes brought up his pole and cast again, this time even further than the first. Austin admired his technique and thought, now that they were friendly, maybe he'd join him out here sometime. "Admiral Vellory was there that night, correct?"

"Sure was. Honored to say he was at my place. Even with circumstances being what they ended up being. Stayed right through to the end of the game."

"What game?" Lucy asked, shooting Austin a look.

"Mariner's game. Played the hated Red Sox that night and McDougal took a no-hitter into the eighth inning. We were all enjoying ourselves. Adam, Hammer and Joey, but Vellory most of all. Huge Mariners guy."

Lucy jotted some lines in her notebook. "What time did the game end?"

"Around ten, ten-thirty."

"Interesting," Austin said. "And you're sure Vellory stayed until the end?"

Bakes nodded. "Don't see why it matters, but yeah."

"We're just trying to put together a timeline of the events that night," Austin said as neutrally as he could. He didn't want to appear too interested. He knew Sy might come to speak with Bakes—if she hadn't already—and he didn't want to clue Bakes into the fact that there was an inconsistency in Vellory's story. He still didn't understand why Sy and her team had shut them out of the case, but, until he did, he wanted to keep their investigation close.

Lucy stepped toward the lake so she was right next to Bakes. "We heard a rumor that Adam Del Guado might have gotten into an argument that night. Any truth to that?"

"Everything I know is in the files," Bakes said. "He was roasting his pals, of course, but no, didn't see any argument. Not *that* night anyway."

Across the lake, a white SUV pulled into the parking lot, stopping right next to Lucy's car. He couldn't make out the driver and couldn't tell if it was Anna's SUV, Sy's SUV, or someone else's. When no one got out, he turned his attention back to Bakes. "You said *that* night. Did Del Guado argue with someone *another* night?"

"Del Guado had come in a couple times before for a beer, maybe some bait." He scratched his beard, thinking. "At some point in the week before he disappeared, I heard him outside arguing with someone. Didn't sound like much, and I reported it after Del Guado disappeared."

"That's not how it came across in the files we read," Lucy said.

Austin agreed. The files only mentioned a vague report of

some argument Del Guado had. They didn't mention that Bakes had heard it or that it had taken place on an entirely different night.

"Don't know nothin' about your files," Bakes said, "but that's what I told 'em at the time."

"Who was he arguing with?" Austin asked.

Bakes shrugged. "Man, that's all I know. You know how the walls in that place are, New York. I was in the dining room and heard some shouting, poked my head out and the argument was already over. Del Guado headed back inside and the man was already leaving."

"What did he look like?" Austin asked.

"Kinda skinny. Brown hair."

Austin saw a head of long, jet black hair emerge from the SUV across the lake. He couldn't make out her face from that distance, but he was sure it was Sy from her tall stature and the elegant way she walked.

Austin nudged Lucy, who looked in Sy's direction just as she disappeared behind a tree. Most likely, Sy was heading around the lake, taking the path that would lead straight to them.

"Thanks for your time, Bakes," Austin said quickly.

Lucy shot him a look.

"We need to head out, Lucy. Bakes, thanks for your time."

Bakes, who didn't seem to mind that their conversation was over, cast his line into the lake and began whistling some classic rock song Austin almost recognized.

Austin led Lucy away from the shore, but not to the path they'd taken to get there. Instead, he took a path that led around the other side of the lake.

When they were thirty yards away, Austin stopped.

Lucy frowned. "What the hell?"

"Sy, from NCIS. She's on her way over. I tried pointing her out."

"So?"

"Remember what Ridley said? We're not supposed to be investigating. Sy finds out and tells Sheriff Daniels..."

Lucy considered this. "Right, right."

Austin thought for a moment. He couldn't believe what he was about to say, but he said it anyway. "You head to the car. I'm going back. Gonna try to listen in."

Lucy frowned. "No."

When he was with the NYPD, he hated sleazy private investigators. Now, well, he could see their side of things. "I know you can't come with me and would never condone what I'm about to do. But... I can't explain it. Sy is up to something, and I need to find out what."

Lucy put her hands on her hips. "If Ridley finds out—or, God forbid, Daniels—I had no prior knowledge."

Austin smiled, "Of course."

And with that, he ducked low and began creeping back along the path toward Bakes, following the sound of his whistling.

PART 2

A FIREHOSE OF LIES

CHAPTER THIRTEEN

THE PROBLEM WAS, the area where Bakes was fishing had been cleared of trees, so Austin could only get to within twenty yards of the spot while remaining hidden.

Standing between two large trees and shielded by a third, he slowly peeked out as Sy approached Bakes, who looked even more annoyed by the second interruption than he had by the first. That was, until he saw who was doing the interrupting. A lifelong bachelor, Bakes was known to be a bit of a ladies man, but the way he looked Sy up and down was like something out of a movie that would never get made nowadays.

Still, Sy handled it like a pro, extending her hand, shaking, then revealing her ID. Austin cursed under his breath. He was too far away to hear their conversation. All he could make out were mumbles and an occasional word.

Peeking out from behind the tree periodically, he watched for five or ten minutes. Finally, Sy shook Bakes' hand and left, but instead of walking back in the direction she'd come, she headed down the path toward Austin. And she was pulling out her cell phone.

For half a second, he considered stepping out from behind

the tree and admitting everything, but something made him freeze. It was curiosity that always came with the familiar taste of the tart cherries he'd been addicted to since he was a child. He had to know what was going on, no matter how ill-advised his methods of finding out.

Back against the tree, he rotated around as Sy came closer, her steps light but audible over the dry leaves.

Then she spoke. "Yeah, I just spoke with him... yup, you were spot on... no, he didn't know anything about that."

She listened for a while, then said, "My read on him is he's a hundred percent above board. Bakes is no genius, but he's not lying, and he's definitely not involved. I believe him when he says he doesn't know anything."

Austin had believed him as well.

"Right, okay," she continued.

"Yeah, we're close to wrapping this thing up," Sy said. "Navy's gonna come out of this thing as clean as it always does."

Austin could hear the leaves and twigs snapping under her feet as she paced. *As clean as it always does.* What did that mean? It definitely implied that they weren't as clean as they should be.

"Right," Sy said. "Right. Yeah."

She went silent for a long time. Austin listened to his own breath along with the gentle breeze and the occasional note from Bakes, who had continued whistling the moment Sy stopped questioning him.

"I understand," she said at last. "Oh, and get this. Daniels ordered his department to let us have this one, to stand down. And guess who was here just before me? That's right. O'Rourke was her name and she was with the PI that LSG made me call. Yeah, *that* one."

She went quiet and Austin could hear her footsteps getting closer underneath the sound of his own breathing. What he was doing wasn't illegal, but it was one of the shadiest things he'd ever done, and he wasn't proud of it.

Still, it had already paid off. *LSG* had to stand for Luke Seymour Garrison, the man his mother knew, whom he'd already assumed had gotten him involved in this in the first place. Why, he still didn't know.

Lucy leaned on the hood of her car, still unable to believe she'd let Austin go through with his plan. She was not supposed to let private citizens break the law. Well, maybe he wasn't actually breaking any laws.

But still. She knew she couldn't justify what Austin was doing because, when she imagined admitting it to Ridley, her cheeks flushed red in shame. She couldn't see Austin from the parking lot, but the fact that he was somewhere over there in the trees made her feel sick.

Her guilty reveries were interrupted by a call from Anna Downey. "Hello, Anna. Break any big stories today?"

"Lucy O-Likes-Being-My-Best-Source, how's it going?"

"It's going fine, Woodward, and no, I do *not* like being your best source. I don't like being a source at all, unless it gets me or the department something."

Anna was breathing hard, like she was out for a jog or pacing like a mad woman. "Lucy, seriously, you're gonna wanna check your email. Something big is about to come out, and I'm offering you the chance to comment. It may stir things up a bit in your neck of the woods."

Lucy's stomach twisted. "Tell me."

"Just read it. Then call me back if you want."

Lucy ended the call and opened her email. Anna had sent her a document, not a link to a published story. Thankfully, whatever it was hadn't yet been published, so there might still be time to squash it, or at least do damage control.

But any relief she felt disappeared when she read the

headline.

Navy Corruption at the Highest Level Covered Up Decades of Bribery, Fraud

~

Just as Austin heard Sy's footsteps reach the tree only a yard away from him, she exclaimed, "I know I said he was good looking, and no, I didn't ask him out!"

Austin smiled. This situation was growing more ridiculous by the moment. Well, at least this indiscretion had now confirmed something else. She *had* been flirting with him.

He was about to step out from behind the tree when her tone changed suddenly. "You didn't tell me that! If it gets out it could... I know it could ruin you, it could ruin me, ruin..." Her tone grew quiet, almost solemn. "It could ruin a lot of things. Damage the whole country."

Her footsteps were growing further and further away, her words turning into a mumble. Austin looked around the tree and saw that she was headed back in the direction of Bakes. She didn't stop to speak with him, but instead hurried back around the way she'd come.

Damage the whole country.

What could that mean?

When she was out of sight, Austin took the long way around the lake and found Lucy sitting in her car. Wisely, Lucy had moved it to the other side of the lot so Sy hadn't seen her when she returned.

Austin was getting ready to apologize for his stunt, but the look on Lucy's face told him something was up. Her head was buried in her phone and, as she read, her expression changed from surprise to shock to sadness.

She didn't say a word.

Shaking her head slowly, she handed Austin the phone.

CHAPTER FOURTEEN

THE PHONE DISPLAYED the draft of an article from Anna Downey. Austin felt a knot of dread tie itself in his stomach as he began reading.

Navy Corruption at the Highest Level Covered Up Decades of Bribery, Fraud

A case of bribery and fraud, dating all the way back to the Persian Gulf War, also known as Operation Desert Storm, has come to light in recent days, calling into question the honor of some of the highest-ranking members of the U.S. Military.

According to three high-ranking sources, who declined to be named because speaking to the media could threaten their careers, Retired Admiral Tom Vellory oversaw an operation from 1986 to 1997 that involved bribery and fraud, earning him and his subordinates millions of dollars.

According to multiple sources, the campaign of corruption involved ship support contractor Byron Defense Marine Asia (BDMA), a Qatari subsidiary of the Byron Marine Group.

Hussein Ali, a Qatari national and chairman of the company, bribed a large number of uniformed officers of the United States Seventh Fleet, including Admiral Vellory, with at least a half million dollars in cash each, plus travel expenses, luxury items, and prostitutes, in return for classified material about the movements of U.S. ships and submarines during the Gulf War, as well as confidential contracting information and information about active law enforcement investigations into Byron Defense Marine Asia.

According to another source, "Ali exploited the intelligence for illicit profit, brazenly ordering his moles to redirect aircraft carriers, ships and subs to ports he controlled in Southeast Asia so he could more easily bilk the Navy for fuel, tugboats, barges, food, water, and sewage removal."

It is important to note that it is common for branches of the U.S. military to contract services with foreign companies during overseas operations. The scandal involves members of the military profiting by illegally offering information to a particular contractor so he could benefit financially, and doing so in exchange for money or other compensation.

The Navy, through BDMA, even employed divers to search harbors for explosives. Vellory, according to multiple sources, authored "Bravo Zulu" memos—which is an informal term for a letter of commendation from the Navy given to civilians who have performed outstanding services—in order to bolster GDMA's credibility for jobs "well done."

One naval source called the accusations, "Perhaps the worst national-security breach of its kind to hit the Navy since the end of the Vietnam War."

Another said, "If proven true, this is a scandal that will rock the Navy, including one of our most-beloved, most-respected Admirals. I am praying this isn't true."

No sources—either official or unofficial—would respond on the record for this story, and Admiral Vellory himself did not reply to repeated requests for comment.

The Navy is said to be investigating the matter, though it is unclear whether any disciplinary actions will be taken, or how many service members were involved.

Austin handed the phone back to Lucy, too stunned to speak.

Lucy said, "I don't want this to be true. I mean, it can't be true, can it?"

Austin said nothing.

Lucy seemed to be thinking out loud, talking through the possibilities. "It says Vellory had declined to comment, which means he knew this story was in the works when he was talking with us."

Austin nodded.

"Remember what Samantha was saying," Lucy continued, "that there was a firehose of disinformation spreading about the case. Maybe this is part of it. Maybe someone is feeding Anna false information so that..."

He didn't say it out loud, but his first thought was that the firehose of disinformation may have been spread specifically to cover up *this* story, assuming people in power knew it was going to come out. Austin remembered when Anna had asked him whether he was hearing anything out of the Navy. He assumed she'd been working on this story for days, possibly longer.

"Whether or not it's true," Lucy continued, "Someone is leaking this to Anna. And they have a reason. I don't know how this is connected to the homicide, but I know it is. There's simply no chance this is a coincidence."

Austin's head spun. Like Lucy, he didn't know how the story related to their case, but if it was true, it was a level of corruption within the Navy that was almost too shocking to believe. Then it struck him.

Damage the whole country.

This is what Sy had been speaking about on the phone.

"I heard part of Sy's call," he said. "Don't know who she was speaking with, but it sounded like she was part of a Navy cover up. Sounded like they were trying to shield Vellory, to keep this story from coming out."

Lucy started the car. "And it's not out. Not yet, anyway. Anna sent it to me for comment, but what the hell would I have to say about this story? I mean, I don't know about this stuff."

As she pulled out of the parking lot, Austin considered this.

"I don't think Anna was asking for a comment. I think she wants protection, but maybe she's too proud to ask for it. This story is big. Big in a way even *she* may not be able to handle. A case like the Holiday Baby Butcher gets lots of national attention, but a story like this gets attention from a whole other kind of person."

"We should go see her."

Austin was already swiping open his phone to make the call.

Anna lived in a little White House in Kingston, a small town about fifteen minutes from Austin's store in Hansville. It had a cute downtown and a drive-on ferry that led across the water to Edmonds, as well as a walk-on ferry that shuttled commuters back and forth to Seattle.

When they approached, Anna was sitting on the front steps, her blond hair lit by the dim light coming from a dusty sconce. The warm day had turned into a chilly night, and she pulled up the collar of her jacket as they reached the bottom of the steps.

As the white-picket gate clicked shut behind them, Lucy jumped right in. "You haven't published that story yet, have you?"

Anna shook her head slowly. She had a faraway look in her eyes, as though she was either tired or concerned. Possibly both. Austin knew her well enough to know that, while she'd be proud of the massive story she'd gotten, she was smart enough to know that a story like this would change her life. Maybe for the better, but maybe not.

"Good," Lucy said. "That's good."

"It's not ready yet," Anna said, standing. She took the three steps down to join them in the yard. Austin had never seen her looking like this. Her usual confidence was absent, replaced by, if not fear, uncertainty at least.

"I can tell from the look on your face," Austin said, "that you know how big of a story you have."

"I do," Anna said. "I didn't really want a comment, Lucy. I want to make a deal."

Lucy folded her arms. "A deal?"

A car sped by on the road in front of the house.

Anna glanced up nervously. "Let's go inside."

All three were silent as they settled in front of Anna's dormant wood stove. Anna took a blue recliner and offered Austin and Lucy the couch.

"This is too serious to mess around with," Lucy said. "Just lay it out."

"Tell me what you know about Vellory," Anna said. "Specifically, does he have any involvement in the triple homicide you're investigating. Is he a suspect? No, wait..." Lucy had shot halfway out of her chair to object, but Anna steamrolled over her. "Tell me those things, one hundred percent off the record, and I'll tell you everything I know, not all of which is in the story."

Lucy glanced at Austin, looking for his opinion. He'd made trades like this with reporters before. As much as it annoyed him to give a reporter anything, sometimes it was necessary because it would benefit his investigation. He said, "It's Lucy's call, ultimately, but here's my thinking. If you can promise with absolute clarity that you won't publish any of what we tell you, and that you won't tell another soul, I think it's a deal. The bottom line is, we're all in over our heads here. Maybe we can help each other out."

Lucy stood and walked to the window, gazing out at the dark street. "This should be Ridley's call, but, at the same time, I don't want to involve him in this. It could end badly, and if someone goes down, I want it to be me." After a long minute, she sat and met eyes with Anna. "Completely off the record? Deep background. You don't tell a soul?"

Anna nodded.

Lucy waved a hand at Austin as if to say, *Go ahead, tell her everything.*

There wasn't much to tell. Austin summarized their interview with Maria Del Guado and her motley crew, as well as their interview with Vellory, including his inconsistency regarding the time he left the Watering Hole. Finally he told her how Sy had tried to box them out of the case.

"So," Anna said when he was through, "I think I was right. I've got no proof, which is why it's not in my story, but my hunch is that the three dead officers—Del Guado, Hammer, and Joey— were somehow involved in Vellory's bribery plot way back when. And, also I have zero proof, I'd bet that their deaths are connected to him."

"It's a leap," Austin said, "but it's where my mind went as well."

"And it seems as though Sy and NCIS are somehow involved in a cover-up," Lucy added.

A thick silence hung over the room.

Lucy's face reflected the concern Austin felt. He knew as well as Lucy and Anna that the plot they were describing was too huge to wrap their minds around quickly.

"So," Anna said, breaking the silence. "Your side of the bargain. Before you ask: yes, the story is true. I was shown documents backing it up, though I had to agree not to mention them in the piece."

She met Austin's gaze, waiting to see whether he'd object.

He believed her, so he didn't.

She continued, "You'll want to know who my sources were, and I won't give names, but I'll give you a direction."

"What good will that do us?" Lucy asked.

Anna leaned forward, elbows on her knees. "For you, the key is: why would someone leak this? Why now?" She stood and grabbed a can of beer from the kitchen, holding it up as she returned. "Anyone want one?"

They shook their heads and Anna pulled back the ring and took a long swig. "I wasn't even reporting this story. I had no idea about it. One day I get calls from three sources, all Navy, all telling the same story. It was *coordinated*."

"Could they be playing you?" Austin asked.

Anna laughed bitterly. "*Of course* they're playing me. But that doesn't mean what they're saying is false. The documents I saw were real. This is *going* to come out because someone wants it to. I'm just the person they chose to be the messenger."

"What do you mean?" Lucy asked.

She sat back in her recliner. "An organization like the Navy drops a story like this for one of two reasons. One: they know it's going to come out anyway and they want to get ahead of it, spin it in their favor. Two: they want to bring someone down. In this case, I'm almost certain it's the first one. This scandal will be so big, it'll stain the whole Navy, not just Vellory. My sense is that some big paper is working on this—the *Times* or the *Post*, most likely—and some genius in the Navy's PR department decided to give it to me because, if *my* editor publishes it, if *my* name is on it, it will be much easier to spin than if it comes out under a more prestigious masthead."

"Makes sense," Austin said. "So the Navy learns that this is going to come out anyway, they feed it to you hoping to be able to shape the narrative before the big papers are able to report it?"

Anna nodded.

Another silence fell over the room.

It was past dinnertime and Austin was starving. Andy had already fed Run, but he needed to get home. "We're not going to get to the bottom of this tonight. Last question: will the story run, and, if so, when?"

Anna pulled her legs up into the recliner, folding one under the other. She looked afraid. "My editor is getting a second opinion. He has friends at the *Seattle Times*. Of course, I want it to run, but I'm not gonna lie: I'm scared as hell."

Lucy stood. "Let's talk first thing in the morning. If it runs and you feel in danger, come hang out at the station."

Anna smiled. "I'm not that much of a wuss. It's not like I think Vellory will send a hitman for me. It's the attention I'm afraid of. This story will be international news." She tossed her hair back playfully. "How will I look on TV?"

She was trying to make light of it, but Austin could understand her nervousness. He wanted to comfort her, but there wasn't anything to say. If the story came out, it would be the biggest of her life. The firehouse of disinformation Samantha had identified would likely be aimed at her.

Lucy moved to the door.

Austin approached Anna, waiting until she met his eyes. "I wouldn't let my editor put it out. Not yet. Not until you find out why they're giving it to you."

Anna said nothing.

"And either way, everything we told you is completely off the record, right?"

Her look was strange, distant. She'd grown cooler ever since their failed date, but this was something different. Something Austin couldn't place.

"You have my word," she said at last.

CHAPTER FIFTEEN

ANNA'S ARTICLE broke at four in the morning.

Austin read it on his phone as soon as he woke up. It had been softened slightly from the version he'd read. The accusations against Vellory were a little more circumspect, but the thrust of it was the same.

He checked the websites of a few of the major news outlets and, as far as he could tell, none had picked up on it yet, but that would change. If Anna was right, she'd only been leaked the story because the big outlets were already working on it. He had no doubt they'd publish big follow-up pieces soon. Vellory was already close to a household name, but he was about to become something much more than that.

At the café, he checked in with Andy, who'd recently hired another sous chef to lighten the burden of the busy summer months. Andy promised he had everything under control.

After grabbing a coffee for the road, Austin packed Run's dog bed, a few of her favorite toys, and a pack of treats, and made the forty-minute drive from Hansville to the Kitsap Sheriff's office.

When he'd arrived home late the previous evening, Run had

been so excited to see him that she leapt into his shin head first, knocking herself back across the kitchen. He'd decided at that moment that he needed to bring her along if he was going to spend another day on the case.

When he arrived, Run led the way into the office, screaming past the front desk and down the hallway, then darting directly into the conference room. Austin had no idea how she'd known which room he was headed for.

When he reached the doorway, it all made sense. Jimmy was eating a bacon and egg sandwich, and she'd followed the scent. Now she sat at his feet, stone still, looking up at him with her wide-eyed, innocent, best-dog-in-the-world face.

Jimmy tossed her a tiny bit of bacon, which she caught out of the air.

"Congratulations seem to be in order," Austin said, sitting next to him.

He looked up, blank-faced.

"Lucy," Austin said. "The engagement?"

"She *told* you about that?"

"I saw the ring."

"We were gonna make a whole announcement later, and we figured no one would notice, not around here anyway." He softened, a big smile spreading across his face. "Thanks, man. You know I'm crazy about her, always have been."

"I know," Austin said. "And I have a follow-up." He pointed at the sandwich. "Did she convince you to start eating carbs?"

Jimmy looked down at the bread, chuckling. "Letting myself go now that I'm spoken for."

Austin laughed. "Right. You might bulge up to eight percent body fat."

Jimmy picked the rest of the egg out of his sandwich and popped it in his mouth, then tossed the remaining bread in the trash. "Not all of us can attract women with our brains, New

York, some of us have to rely on muscles. But seriously..." he leaned in... "keep the engagement on the DL for now."

"DL?"

"Down low. In humans-under-forty speech it means, 'Don't tell anyone.'"

Austin nodded as Samantha and Ridley walked in, trailed by Lucy.

Ridley took his usual spot in front of the white board as Samantha projected a copy of Anna's article onto the wall. To Austin's surprise, Ridley's lips had a slight upturn to them. Not a smile, but not a frown, which is what he'd expected.

"What is it about Kitsap County's own Anna Downey," Ridley began, "that she finds herself at the center of stories this big?"

Jimmy was shaking his head. "She's never been at the center of a story *this* big."

"Few have," Ridley agreed. "But for now, we need to figure out how it relates to us." He turned to Austin. "Lucy filled me in on your conversations with the victims' families and Vellory."

Austin noticed that Lucy hadn't told him about their conversation with Anna. "You make any progress with the Navy?" Austin asked.

"Zero," Jimmy chimed in. "Turns out our fearless leader has as much clout in Bremerton as I did in high school."

Samantha cocked her head. "I always took you for a popular dumb jock type."

"Believe it or not," Jimmy shot back, "I was an above-average student who just happened to have the physique of a Greek God. It's only around you geniuses that I'm the dumb one."

Ridley ignored their back and forth, as he often did. "With the Navy, there's no way of knowing whether they're stonewalling because they can, or because they're hiding something, or just because that's how large bureaucracies work. In any case, we got nowhere."

"So, where does that leave us regarding the triple?" Lucy asked.

Ridley tapped on the whiteboard with a dry erase marker. "Leaves us wondering how the murder of those three men is connected to Vellory, and this corruption, assuming Anna's story is true."

Samantha rapped her knuckles on the table. "Am I the only one thinking the obvious? Vellory killed them to cover up his crimes back in the day. Maybe they found out about it and confronted him, and he took them out. After all, he was with them that night. Somehow he lured them out to the Bluff and, bang!"

"You're not the only one thinking it," Ridley said, "you're just the only one willing to say it out loud."

"Why would he kill two of them with a rifle and one of them with an obscure Russian pistol?" Austin asked.

No one spoke for a long time. No one could answer because there *was* no good answer. Samantha's theory wasn't crazy, but it didn't fit with what little they knew of the crime scene.

"Confusion," Jimmy finally offered, weakly. "Just to make it look weird." He shook his head. "Nah, I don't even buy that. And I honestly don't buy that Vellory killed them."

"What about the Sy angle?" Lucy asked. "It seems like she may be part of a cover-up. I'm wondering whether we might be dealing with different factions of the Navy. One that's trying to bring Vellory down by leaking the story, another that's trying to cover for him."

Austin pressed his hands into his temples. His head felt like it was going to burst. Run, apparently sensing his stress, leapt up into his lap and curled up.

"I've got something else," Samantha said. "It's not much, but my grandpa served in Desert Storm."

"Wait," Ridley said, "I'm trying to wrap my head around the

fact that you're young enough to have a *grandpa* who served in a conflict only thirty years ago."

"*Anyway*," Samantha continued. "I showed him Anna's article and he offered up one big shrug. He said corruption was everywhere during that war, and that it was even worse in Vietnam. Basically acted like it was no big deal. Told me, 'War is hell. Stuff goes down.'"

"It may be no big deal to him," Lucy said. "But it will be to the country, and it is to me. Small amounts of shadiness to get the job done is one thing, but one of our most-respected Admirals spending a decade getting rich off bribes, that's different."

"True enough," Samantha conceded. "And I did look into Vellory. Ran my AI through message boards, news articles, and so on. The usual spots. Turns out there have been rumors about him being corrupt for twenty years, but just like with the triple homicide, there's a fountain of disinfo out there as well."

"Someone is flooding the zone with BS," Ridley said.

"Yeah," Samantha agreed, "I—" Her eyes fell to her laptop and she stopped suddenly. "Guys..."

"What is it?" Austin asked.

"Her story just changed." Samantha pointed at the wall, where Anna's article was still projected. "The piece just got an update, and it now seems to quote some of the people in this room."

CHAPTER SIXTEEN

FOR THIRTY SECONDS, everyone read in silence. Then Ridley shoved his hands in his pockets and looked at the group, mouth half open in shock, eyes full of anger.

Austin's tongue tingled with the taste of scotch bonnet peppers. His throat burned and his ears grew hot. This was how he experienced rage.

Finally, Ridley managed to speak. "Who? How? Why?"

Anna's article had been updated to include everything they'd spoken about off the record, everything she'd promised *not* to publish. Though it didn't cite Austin or Lucy by name, it included quotes from them regarding their investigation into Vellory, citing "detectives and investigators within the Kitsap Sheriff's Department."

Lucy stood up. "I... I..."

"You *gave* her this?" Ridley bellowed.

Austin stood, Run leaping from his lap and hurrying to the corner. "We both spoke with her last night. She promised..."

"This is bad," Jimmy said.

"Very bad," Samantha added.

Austin fell back into his chair. "She said..."

"Lemme explain," Lucy said, walking over to Ridley, hands out like she was trying to make a peace offering. "We spoke a hundred percent off the record. She told us about her sources and we told her... oh, God."

"You told her every damn thing about our investigation!" Ridley thrust a finger at the article projected onto the wall. "She seems to know even more than me. You didn't tell me about the discrepancy in Vellory's story. The 8PM, 10PM thing."

"We were getting to that," Lucy said, meekly.

Ridley had every right to be angry, but Austin couldn't let her take the brunt of it. "It's my fault," Austin said. "I trusted Anna. I... I still can't believe she would betray us this way."

"I thought you were *dating* her," Ridley said.

"We had one date. It didn't go well."

"So she lured you in, and this is payback or something? You scorned her so she's burning you, burning all of us?"

Austin shook his head. "I don't know. I'd prefer not to believe that."

Run ran over to Jimmy and hopped in his lap. She could probably sense the change in Austin's mood, and Jimmy calmed her down by feeding her tiny bits of bacon that had fallen onto the table.

Ridley continued. "This is going to alert NCIS that we're still working the case, alert Vellory that we're looking into him. Not to mention, when Daniels hears about this..."

"We screwed up," Lucy said. "We trusted her and..." she let her arms go wide. "Boss, how can we fix this?"

After leaving messages on Anna's phone, and with her editor, Austin left Run with Jimmy and drove Samantha to the Best Buy

ten minutes from the office. There was no fixing their screw-up.
For now, there was nothing to do but wait until the fallout hit
them.

"You want to tell me what this is about?" Samantha asked,
standing in front of a display of laptops.

"Not especially."

"Your wife, I'm assuming."

Austin nodded. "I'd rather not say more. Can you tell me,
why would a person send me the instructions the way they did?"

Samantha selected a laptop. "Six hundred bucks okay?"

Austin nodded and they headed to the checkout.

"It's easy," Samantha said. "Anonymity. A new laptop
purchased at a random store means no tracking software has
been pre-installed. That is, not counting all the tracking software the companies install on these things to serve you ads."

Austin swiped his credit card, struck with an odd feeling. For
nearly two years he'd lived with Fiona's murder. At one time he'd
imagined himself solving it by pounding the pavement in New
York City. Now, here he was in a city three-thousand miles away
with a woman half his age explaining online security.

Laptop box tucked under his arm, they walked out. It was
late morning and the fog had burned off, the hot sun beating
down on them. Silverdale often ran ten degrees hotter than
Hansville, but even for June, today was unreasonably hot.

"And the rest of it?" Austin asked. "The browser, the app?"

"Same," Samantha said. "Just security. Tor browser doesn't
track activity like the normal ones do. The VPN is so your IP
address can't be traced, and the video app he told you to get is
just like Signal, the text app he had you download. End-to-end
encryption. But with video instead of messages."

Austin stopped and looked at her over the hood of his truck.
"So when I get home tonight and set this up, and when I finally
video chat with this guy, it'll be untraceable, unhackable?"

Samantha chuckled. "Nothing is unhackable. But the smartest people I know would have a tough time listening in on your chat. Whoever this person is knows what they're doing, and knows they want to speak in private."

Ridley ushered Austin into his private office as soon as he got back. "Remember when I first asked you to come in, and Daniels ripped us apart after that whole chase through Kingston?"

"Ahhh, precious memories," Austin joked, looking for humor, for anything to feel good about. His anger at Anna had died down, settling into confusion. For the life of him, he couldn't understand why she'd burnt them the way she had.

Ridley was unamused. "That conversation with Daniels was a milkshake at the local soda shop compared to what's about to happen."

Austin swallowed the lump in his throat. "He heard about Anna's new article?"

Ridley nodded and pulled out one of the two chairs behind his desk. "Have a seat, New York. You're about to catch a flaming crap sandwich."

"Happy to, but what do you mean?"

"This case, this story, is getting out of control. I don't know where it goes, but I need to protect Lucy. There's a chance my career doesn't survive this. That your reputation doesn't." He leveled his gaze on Austin, saying more with his eyes than he had with his words. "I need Lucy to come out of this unscathed."

What he was saying was that he wanted Austin to take all the blame for the quotes in Anna's article, and that he himself would take all the blame for the investigation happening in the first place. "Understood," Austin said.

Ridley opened up his video chat and dialed. A moment later,

Sheriff Daniels appeared on screen against the backdrop of a hotel room, complete with cheesy art and extra-thick curtains.

"Boss, I'm here with Austin." Ridley adjusted the computer so Austin was in the picture with him.

Daniels was red-faced and bleary-eyed, causing Austin to wonder whether his sobriety had been short-lived. As much as he disliked the man, he didn't want to be the cause of a fall off the wagon.

"You two," Daniels said, shaking his head. "You two. I have half a mind to... Do you know who I just spoke with? I could give you a hundred guesses and you'd never get it."

Austin thought about throwing out a smart-ass comment, but decided against it.

"The Secretary of the Navy," Daniels continued, "from D.C. Do you know how bad things have to be for him to call a nobody like me? That man eats breakfast with the president once a month."

"Did he threaten you?" Ridley asked.

"Threaten? Men like that control armies that could topple small countries before lunch. That could win World War Three. You think he needs to *threaten* me? I had to hit the mini-bar just to take the call. That man could end my career with a single text message. How do you think he felt about my officers telling a reporter that we're investigating their most-beloved Admiral?"

"I'm sorry," Austin said. "Allow me to say: the quotes in the updated version of the article were from me, and they were given on the understanding that they were off the record. It was a trade to get information that could help us solve the case."

Daniels kicked out his chair and began pacing the hotel room, coming and going from the frame. Finally, he leaned into the camera, his red face growing big on their screen. "A case you were NOT supposed to be investigating." He sat down, more defeated than angry. "Austin, Ridley, do you remember when you were working on the Baby Butcher case. In my office, Austin, you said, 'When lives are on the line, I make the rules.' Do you remember that?"

Austin nodded. Ridley and others had mocked him for that for months.

Daniels shook his head. "You're an arrogant bastard, Austin. When it's chasing a suspect through my streets, that's one thing. This one... this is national security... this is..." He let his head fall into his hands. "This is bad."

Ridley said, "If I might. I know we were supposed to leave this to NCIS, but boss, a triple homicide occurred in our county. It was colder than a popsicle in the back of the freezer until a few days ago." He stood, leaning his taut face into the camera, his voice rising. "I understand there are national ramifications here, but you put three bodies in front of me in my backyard, I'm gonna try to solve it unless and until the president himself shows up and tells me to stand down."

"*I'm* your boss and I'm ordering you to stand down. Leave this to NCIS, to the Navy. Or you're fired."

Austin stared at Ridley, whose face quivered. "Rid," he whispered, "back off."

Slowly, Ridley leaned back. His face tightened and he jabbed a finger at the screen. His mouth opened, but nothing came out.

Finally, his chest dropped and he let out a long sigh. "Back off, got it, Sheriff." Before Daniels could reply, he closed his laptop, ending the call.

Austin was stunned. Too stunned to say something snarky. "Rid, I hate to say it, but..."

"Stop, Austin. Just stop. Lemme think." Ridley stood and walked to the window, where he picked up a picture of Rachel, his wife, wearing a yellow summer dress and standing in front of their home. "I know that technically I can't order you around. You're a consultant. But I'll make this request, and I'll tell the same to Lucy and the others. Do not stand down. Do not back off."

"But Rid…"

"If Daniels comes back, I don't want him to be able to say that Lucy or the others disobeyed my command. This all falls on me. Go out and solve this thing, even if it means bringing down the entire U.S. Navy, and everyone in it."

CHAPTER SEVENTEEN

AN HOUR LATER, Austin watched Lucy emerge from Ridley's office, her face hard, determined. She pulled Austin into the conference room, where Run had gotten herself a snack from the table. Apparently someone's abandoned muffin had been too much of a temptation and, after polishing off what was left of the snack, she'd decided to shred the plate to destroy the evidence.

"Did you need a treat?" Austin said.

Run looked up at him without remorse. She didn't often behave poorly, but nothing drove her like abandoned food. Austin fixed her a little bowl of water and set some treats on her bed in the corner. Run lapped up the water before laying down as Austin picked up the bits of paper.

Jimmy came back into the room holding a cup of coffee, followed by Samantha, who had hit a new personal record: she now carried three different laptops.

"We still haven't reached Anna," Lucy said, "though I don't think it'll do much good when we do. We can't put the toothpaste back in the tube." She noticed Samantha's triple-laptop setup. "Why three? Is it some security relay thing?"

"Nah," Samantha said, "I feel better when I'm surrounded by more firepower. She plugged one of them into the projector. "I have new information on Vellory. That guy is crooked as a pig's... um... reproductive organ."

She tapped some keys on her laptop. On the wall, an article came up.

"Whoa," Jimmy said, "this is no longer a local story."

It was an article from the *New York Times*, and Samantha didn't even give them time to read it before she clicked over to another article, this one from the *Washington Post*. Then another, from Fox. "The articles are all quite similar," she said. "And all similar to Anna's."

Austin scanned the article. "Nothing new there," he said. "Confirms Anna's story, at least." As confused as he was about why she'd done it, part of him felt glad for her. Being out on a limb as the only reporter in the country with a story like this would be lonely, and possibly dangerous. Now that multiple big outlets had confirmed her scoop, she was in a much better position.

"Here's what's new," Samantha said. "About an hour ago, documents started leaking onto Reddit... which I can tell from your blank stare, Austin, you've never heard of."

He shrugged.

"It's an app and website, message board, kinda like Facebook, but anonymous. Avatars instead of photos of yourself, all kinds of different discussion communities." She clicked and a document popped up. On the top, in bright red lettering, it was stamped *Confidential*.

It looked like a receipt for fuel, tens of thousands of gallons.

Samantha clicked, and the image on the wall changed to a photograph of a scantily clad woman, walking arm-in-arm with a man in uniform, whose face was blacked out.

Austin's mouth dropped open.

"What the what?" Jimmy said.

"That's right," Samantha said. "That's Admiral Tom 'TV' Vellory, with what I assume is a high priced sex worker, circa 1991. And there are hundreds more images and documents leaking." She paused for effect. She was clearly enjoying herself. "Everything in the *Times* article, the *Post* article, Anna's article. It's all proven unequivocally by these leaks."

"Who's leaking it?" Austin asked.

Samantha shrugged. "The documents are being leaked on Reddit from dozens of different accounts."

Austin stood and did a lap around the conference table. His mind raced with possibilities. "Could be a foreign government trying to embarrass the U.S. Could be people who tried to blackmail Vellory, or the Navy, to keep the story quiet. Could be... well, there are too many options."

"You didn't let me get to the good part," Samantha said. "And by *good*, I mean tragic."

She clicked, and another image popped up. Austin recognized the face of Jack Hammeron, Hammer, one of the deceased. The photo was taken from far away, through the window of a café, and he sat with a man who appeared to be middle eastern, with olive skin and a long black beard.

"According to this leak," Samantha said, "That's Hussein Ali, the guy who bribed Vellory, the mastermind of this whole scandal."

Jimmy stood up. "Meeting directly with one of our victims."

Samantha clicked again. A scrawled letter popped up. "This is from Joey Blake to Ali, thanking him for the 'amazing night in Dubai' and asking for the name of the call girl he spent the evening with." Her face showed as much disgust as Austin felt. "If I showed up in Hollywood with a script of this story, they'd send me out of the room because it was too ridiculous." She closed her laptop. "And there's more. Stuff on Adam Del Guado and half a dozen other service members. A lot of people were involved in this fraud. And it all leads back to Vellory."

Lucy shook her head. "I can't believe I had a poster of that guy on my wall."

There was a knock at the door and everyone looked up at once as it creaked open.

Austin frowned, leaning back when he saw who it was.

Anna's slacks were wrinkled, her hair tied into a messy bun, her eyes tired. "Austin, Lucy, can I speak with you in private?"

Austin shut the door behind them and sat across from Anna in the private room at the end of the hall. The place smelled of stale coffee and mildew, like it needed a good airing out.

Lucy leaned against the wall in the corner, unable to look directly at Anna. "Why?" was all she said.

"First," Anna said, "I'm sorry."

"Sorry?" Austin scoffed. "Sorry?"

"Let me explain, please. It wasn't my fault." Anna dropped her face and laced her hands in her lap. She looked like she might cry.

Austin folded his arms. "Go ahead."

Anna finally looked up. "My editor had the first story, the original version. The one I showed you, but softened up a bit." She sighed. "I *always* write up my notes in a document, even for off-the-record conversations. Just for my own personal use. Sometimes I go over them with my editor. In this case, I filed the final version of the story and went to sleep. Next morning, I slept in, went for a walk, trying to clear my head. When I came back, he'd already taken my notes, the quotes you gave me, and added them to the story."

"Why would he do that?" Austin asked.

"I added the notes from our conversation to the wrong document. I put my notes from our off-the-record talk into my regular notes file, which he has access to, instead of the OTR file that's private to me." She looked up, imploring him with her eyes, then she looked at Lucy. "I have never, ever burned a source like I burned you guys. I am sorry, even though I know that doesn't help things. I alerted Vellory to your investigation, and I don't even know what other harm I caused."

She stood and walked to the door. "I can't take it back, but I wanted you to know that it was an accident. I really am sorry."

She didn't wait for a response.

CHAPTER EIGHTEEN

SY'S DAY had been long and not especially fun. All she wanted was to get home, have dinner, and tune out in front of the TV, but she had to make one more stop.

She parked at the Poulsbo Safeway, which was on the way home, and grabbed a cart. Her fridge was empty and this was going to be a long week. She'd gone days munching on almonds and a sad bag of mini-carrots from her vegetable drawer, but if she was going to get through this case, she needed real food.

She grabbed fruit, a loaf of bread, a few frozen dinners, a tub of premade macaroni and cheese, and finally some coffee and milk. She was headed for the checkout stand when her phone rang.

She cursed under her breath when she saw the caller-ID. It was Benny Ramirez, a young investigator on her team who wouldn't take no for an answer.

She stepped over to the corner, leaning on the cold case full of milk. "Benny?"

"Hey boss, quick thing. Like you said, I buried myself in the files, and I might have found something."

"I told you that to get you out of my hair, Benny. I didn't

want you to actually *find* anything. Like I said, this thing is being handled elsewhere."

He paused, probably unsure how to respond. "Okay, but you saw the articles about Vellory, right?"

Benny was a smart kid. Well, at twenty-three or so, he wasn't a kid, but he seemed like a kid to her. Enthusiastic, optimistic, and always ready to take on the next task. But he hadn't yet learned that sometimes the internal politics of a situation were more important than the normal procedures. "Like I told you," Sy said, "leave him alone. There are things here above our pay grades. He wasn't involved in the murders."

"Back in ninety-two, he said he left the bar at eight. In your notes from when you went out there the other day, he said he left at ten."

"Stop it, Benny. That's an order."

"Sy, you know I respect the hell out of you, but I don't understand. Everything is pointing at this guy being guilty and—"

"Benny, I—" She cut herself off when a young mother pushed past her with a double stroller, trying to get to the milk. "I can't be having this chat here," she continued. "Just trust me, there's more going on that you don't know about and..." her phone vibrated. Call waiting. "Benny, I gotta go."

She took a deep breath. This was the call she'd been waiting for. "Captain Garrison. Thanks for calling me back."

"Sorry it took a while. Things have been busy, as I'm sure you can understand."

"I did what you asked, sir."

"I know, and I appreciate it."

She was expecting more, an explanation of some sort. It wasn't often that people at Garrison's level asked her for favors, so when he'd asked her to invite Austin along when she visited the crime scene, she'd been happy to oblige, knowing the favor would likely come back to her at some point.

She cleared her throat. "If I might ask, why did you want

Austin brought along to begin with? You know, we've shut the locals out of this case completely now. It was a bit of a tease. And, he seemed smart and all, but he really didn't bring anything to the table that we didn't have."

"I asked a favor, you did it. Can we just leave it there?" Garrison sounded annoyed.

She made her way down the aisle, phone tucked under her chin.

"You seem like the curious type, but also the career-oriented type, Sy."

"I am, sir. I find they often go together."

"Sometimes, they're at odds."

She thought for a moment, choosing her words carefully. "Sometimes they are. Is this one of those times?"

Garrison was quiet for a moment. "Fine. And I'm only telling you this because a lot of decent people are going to be brought down in the coming weeks and months. A lot of scandals. A lot of ruined careers, some deservedly so. I don't want you thinking I'm involved in any of the truly salacious stuff. I asked you to invite Austin for *personal* reasons. I used to, well, *know* his mother. I wanted to have an excuse to call her. To get her to call me back."

Sy stopped. "*Know* her? Like, when she was married?"

"I trust you can keep it quiet?"

"Sure, but..."

"I didn't want you thinking it had anything to do with the Vellory situation."

"I didn't. I—"

"Of course you did. Like you said, you're curious."

With that, he ended the call.

She couldn't believe what had just happened. Garrison had asked her to involve Austin in the case so he'd have something to discuss with Austin's mother, with whom he'd had an affair decades ago. Sometimes she'd wished she'd gone into a line of work that didn't involve as much politics.

Sy waited for a moment, planning what she'd say, then dialed the cell phone of Thomas Austin.

CHAPTER NINETEEN

AUSTIN'S PHONE vibrated on the table and he picked it up, surprised and intrigued. "Sy, to what do I owe this unexpected call?"

"Will you have dinner with me tonight?"

Austin surveyed the landscape of Chinese takeout food spread over the conference table. In the corner, Jimmy was using a fork to pick the beef out of a noodle dish, careful to avoid too many carbs, while Lucy and Samantha passed containers back and forth. Run stared up at them, waiting for scraps.

"Dinner tonight doesn't work," he said. "What's this about?"

"Can't a girl ask a guy to dinner anymore without getting the third degree?"

Austin walked into the hallway to avoid the prying eyes of the others. "You're asking me out on a date, or to talk business? I mean, the way you shut down Ridley made me think I'd never hear from you again." He'd almost said "*see* you again," but that made him think about his shenanigans in the woods, which he was still embarrassed about.

"It's not a date," she said. "And it's not business. It's a little of both."

Austin considered this. But before he could respond, she said, "C'mon, there's an Italian place near my house that'll put your best culinary efforts to shame."

"That sounds like a challenge. But really, I'm about to eat, and I'm working."

"Working on the case you're not supposed to be working on?"

Austin paced the hallway. "I'm not at liberty to say."

He found himself skeptical of her every word, but if she was working some angle, for the life of him he couldn't figure out what it was.

"Fine," she said. "Make me a counter offer."

"Breakfast, my café. Tomorrow at eight." The words came out before he knew what he was saying.

"I'll be there."

She ended the call and Austin made his way back into the conference room. He could tell the three of them had been discussing him by the way they all went silent as soon as he walked in.

Samantha laughed. "You know how thin these walls are, New York?"

"Was that Sy?" Lucy demanded.

"Please tell me that was Sy," Jimmy said, a wide grin across his face. "I've never met her, but I Googled her and—"

Lucy tossed a balled up napkin at his head. "You really don't want to finish that sentence."

Jimmy raised his palms defensively. "I was going to say she strikes me as an intelligent, caring, professional woman."

"That was Sy," Austin admitted. "I'm having breakfast with her tomorrow. I can't figure out what's going on, but I'm fairly sure she's not coming just to try our new breakfast sandwich."

Austin's phone vibrated again, but this time it was a number he didn't recognize. "Hello?"

"Uhh, is this, um... Thomas something... Thomas, uhh,

Austin?" The voice was a man's, and it was shaky, uncertain. But it was also familiar.

"It is."

"This is Jack Hammeron, Junior. I met you the other day at Maria Del Guado's house."

Austin waved a hand to quiet down the others, who still seemed to be having a laugh at his expense.

"Hammer Junior," Austin said. "Thanks for calling. Yes, we met. How can I help you?"

There was a long silence on the line, amplified by the silence in the room. Lucy, Jimmy, and Samantha had noticed the name when he'd said it aloud.

"Well, I've called a few others. Honestly, you're my last call."

"Um, okay," Austin said.

"You said to call if I thought of anything else."

Austin stood. "Absolutely."

"You know how you have these seemingly random memories, and as an adult you don't know *why* you remember them?"

"I do know about that." Austin said. As eager as he was to hear what Hammer Junior was calling about, he wanted to make a connection first. "For me, it's this swing set in Connecticut. Sometimes when I'm walking down a flight of stairs, I randomly remember it. Nothing special about that swing set, and I have no idea why I remember it when I walk down stairs. Some glitch in my wiring, I guess."

Hammer Junior laughed. A good sign. Austin remembered his hard stare and sour demeanor. He'd had would-be sources call him and then have second thoughts and clam up. Sometimes the best way to get someone talking was to seem uninterested, or at least not desperate.

"Yeah," Hammer Junior said, "it's like that. So I read some articles, all the stuff coming out about Vellory. And I saw the stuff on Reddit. They're saying my dad was part of it. You know anything about that?" His voice had grown quieter, sadder.

"Not much more than you. I don't think we know if that's true, but if it is, I'm sorry. And if it isn't, I'm sorry about the rumors."

"I won't lie... I think it's all true. Mom didn't tell me everything, but I think she knew he came home from Desert Storm with extra cash."

"I'm sorry," Austin said.

Hammer Junior sighed. "If he made some extra cash while he was over there, well... I don't know what I think about that." He paused, as though thinking it through. "That's not why I'm calling, though. It was something else my mom said. I remembered it yesterday as I was walking through a Wal-Mart parking lot. Just randomly."

Austin held his breath.

"She said she didn't like when dad went out to Hansville to hang out because once he'd had a run in with a guy there, an ex-Seal."

"Did she say anything else?"

"You know how parents sometimes sugarcoat things to kids? Well, I think she was sugarcoating it. You saw my size, right? My dad was even bigger. I'm literally the runt of the litter at six foot three, two thirty."

Austin considered what he was saying. "So if your mom told you he had a run-in with a guy..."

"That meant they fought, and she was worried they'd fight again."

"Any idea what they fought about?"

"Adam. Mr. Del Guado. She said it had to do with him."

Austin paced the room, Run's eyes following him like he might be holding a T-bone steak. "Did she say anything else you recall?"

"That's it. Could that be helpful? I called that other woman, Symone or whatever, but she never called me back."

"It might be helpful," Austin said, "and I'll pass this along to the right people. And please don't hesitate to call if you remember anything else."

Austin ended the call and dug into the food, dishing himself a plate of white rice and kung pow chicken.

Lucy raised an eyebrow in his direction. "What was that about?"

Before he could answer, a man's face appeared on the wall, projected from one of Samantha's laptops. Samantha looked triumphant. "It was about *this* guy."

Austin was stunned. "How did you..."

"I overheard Hammer Junior," she said. "Austin, you really need to go outside if you want anything resembling privacy."

Austin frowned.

"It's just my nature," she continued. "He mentioned an ex-Seal living in Hansville, which has a population of like four thousand. This guy popped right up." She smiled. "And he's got a bit of a sheet." She paused. "Grand theft auto, assault, assault again. Dude had the grit to become a Seal—not an easy get—and was dishonorably discharged for insubordination."

The picture was the mugshot of a white guy, maybe thirty-five years old, with greasy brown hair. "How old is the picture?" Austin asked.

"From his arrest in 2002."

Austin studied the face. He looked like... no, he *was* the man Austin had tossed off his property for harassing Anna. "I know that guy. Davey Wragg. He was at my store. He's... oh, no."

Lucy was right there with him. "The note in the file about the confrontation Adam had with another man."

"The argument confirmed by Bakes," Austin added. "Ten to one says it was with that guy. And Hammer Junior just told me that Hammer had a confrontation with him as well. Sounds like it was an ongoing thing."

"Okay," Jimmy said, standing. "It's nine o'clock at night. How do we approach it?"

Austin sat and kicked his feet up in a spare chair and grabbed his phone. "Well, I banned him for life from my place. How about I call and kindly offer to unban him?"

It took Samantha longer to find his phone number than it had to find his file and mugshot.

She handed Austin a slip of paper. "No cell phone, at least not that I can find. Landline for his place out in Hansville, which he shares with a roommate named Damian, according to the magic internet research I just did."

Austin was already dialing.

After five long rings, a sleepy voice came on the line. "Um, hello?"

"May I speak with David Wragg?" Austin asked, as politely as he could manage.

"Davey ain't here."

"Oh, I'm sorry to hear that. Do you know where he is?"

The man on the other end of the line chuckled bitterly. "Who knows with that dude? He's a month late on rent already, promised it to me today, and now he disappears?"

"Disappears?" Austin asked. "Did he say where he was going?"

"Said something about a rare gun show in Tacoma."

The hair on the back of Austin's neck prickled. *Rare gun show.*

Samantha was typing furiously on her laptop. "Buy some time," she whispered.

"Am I speaking with his roommate, Damian?" Austin asked.

"Who *is* this?"

"Any idea when he'll be back?" Austin asked.

"No." The guy was clearly pissed.

Samantha whispered. "There's no rare gun show going on in Tacoma. At least not one that's public."

Austin looked at Lucy, who signaled for him to wrap up the call. "Okay, thanks," Austin said.

The guy hung up without another word.

Lucy was already headed for the door. "Nice job, New York. That guy sounded surprised to get a call, and he'll be even more surprised when we show up at his door."

CHAPTER TWENTY

DAVEY WRAGG and his roommate lived at the end of a little dirt road not far from Buck Lake, where Austin had met Bakes and eavesdropped on Sy a few days earlier. The headlights of Lucy's car leapt from road to trees as it bounced over divots in the road. A mix of dust and fog rose up before them, giving the night a haunted, eerie feeling.

On the ride over, Austin had accomplished three things. First, he'd gotten Anna to send him the picture from Davey Wragg's dating profile. They still hadn't addressed the tension left between them from the article, but her help was a good first step in thawing out the iciness. Next, he'd sent the photo to Samantha who, with Ridley's approval, had sent it out to every officer in the state. They didn't have anything solid on the guy, but the hunt for Davey Wragg was on. At the very least, he needed to come in and answer some questions. Finally, Austin had convinced Lucy to call Ridley and beg him to pull every string he could to get a wiretap on Wragg's mother's phone. She lived in a retirement community in East Seattle, so Ridley would have to ask for help from his colleagues across the water, but Austin knew he could get it done. Reluctantly, he'd agreed.

Austin was fairly sure Wragg's roommate hadn't been lying about him not being there, but they weren't going to take any chances. Jimmy was following close behind them in his patrol car.

They parked out front and, lit by the headlights of both cars, the house appeared to be in poor shape, but it was larger than Austin had imagined. Three cement steps led to a screen door, which opened as they got out of the car.

"Stop!" Lucy shouted, her hand dropping to her firearm. "Kitsap police."

On the top step, a man's hands shot up, his pants sagging as though he'd been holding them up in lieu of a belt.

"Don't shoot!" he called, his voice full of fear. "I only came out to see who it was." Austin recognized the voice. It was Damian, the roommate he'd spoken with.

"Keep your hands up," Lucy said.

"My pants are falling down. I don't have any underwear on."

It was true. With each second his hands were up, his pants dropped another quarter inch, slowly sliding down his hips.

Jimmy rushed forward, quickly patted him down, then told him to drop his hands and pull up his pants.

As Lucy and Austin approached the porch, Jimmy tried to reassure the terrified man. "You're not in any trouble," he said. "At least, I don't think so. We came to ask about Davey."

Damian pushed open the screen door. "Did I speak with you on the phone?"

"You spoke with me," Austin said, "and we appreciate your help."

Leading them into a filthy living room, he waved at a couch half-covered with magazines about antique dolls. "Just push all that out of the way."

"Is anyone else in the house?" Jimmy asked.

"N- No. You can check if you w- want." Damian's face was shaking.

Jimmy did a quick check of the house, then returned. "All clear."

Austin could tell that Damian was too terrified to lie.

"Doll collector?" Austin asked, holding up one of the magazines.

Despite his thick hooded sweatshirt and pants being pulled up, Damian was shaking like he'd spent a day outside naked in the snow. "Can't afford anything good. I just like to look at them."

"There's nothing to be afraid of," Austin said, stacking up the magazines and sitting on the couch.

Lucy and Jimmy showed Damian their badges and explained that Austin was a police consultant, helping them on an important case, then Lucy sat next to Austin. Jimmy posted up along the wall, arms folded, eyes darting from door to door, just in case.

Lucy then looked to Austin, and Austin offered a little wave toward Damian, as if to say, *He's all yours.* He and Lucy had spoken with a few suspects and witnesses together by this point, and sometimes a shared sixth sense told them who'd have better luck with a particular interviewee. In this case, Austin was quite sure Damian had nothing to do with the case—other than the bad luck of being Davey Wragg's roommate—and he thought Lucy's lighter touch might be in order.

"So," Lucy began, "There are no gun shows going on in Tacoma right now. Davey lied about where he was going."

Damian was in his late-thirties or early-forties, Austin thought, but his face had a youthful look, his skin tanned, like he got more sun than the average Washingtonian. His blue eyes darted from Austin to Lucy. "But *I* didn't lie. I swear that's what he told me."

"Damian, ya gotta settle down, bro." Jimmy was trying to sound friendly, but his folded arms and gratuitous muscles were likely intimidating.

Lucy shot him a look, then continued. "Why would he lie, do you think?"

Damian closed his eyes tight, as though he could make it all go away. "He's a dirtbag. Really. I'm embarrassed to live with him. I used to live in a nice place in Kingston, commuted to Seattle every day. Lost my job and had to take the first place I could get. My name isn't even on the lease here and he's constantly trying to stick me with the bills."

"Did he say anything else about where he might be? Does he have friends or family that you know of?"

"He often disappears for a few days at a time, comes back smelling weird, like tar or concrete or something. I know he hunts, if that helps. I'm a Second Amendment guy, but he's something else. Total gun nut."

Bingo, Austin thought.

Lucy was easing into it. "Yes, does he keep any firearms in the house?"

Damian nodded. "A few that I know of. When he left the other day, he had a few rifle cases with him."

"What sorts of guns does he collect?" Lucy asked.

"Okay, get this," Damian said. He seemed to be relaxing now that he was sure he wasn't in any trouble, and he had a good, free flowing storytelling style. "First day I move in, I'm making small talk. You know: where did you grow up, what are your hobbies? He goes into his room and brings out a small black gun case. Opens it and stares at me like he's showing me a case of gold, or evidence of the Loch Ness Monster."

"What was in the case?" Lucy asked, shifting to the edge of the couch.

"Some old gun he thought was special. Like I said, I support gun rights, but I don't give a crap about some old Russian pistol."

Old Russian pistol. The murder weapon.

"Do you know if he took that one with him?" Lucy asked casually.

"He did. I mean, feel free to check his room, but I think he took everything."

CHAPTER TWENTY-ONE

THE CAFÉ WAS QUIET, but would likely be filling up over the next hour or two. Austin loved the quiet mornings when it was only him, Run, Andy, and a few customers.

He'd gotten home exhausted, then woken up early and taken Run for a jog on the beach. He'd never been a great athlete, but he'd been in better shape when he was in the NYPD, and was determined that this was the summer he'd get back there. A twenty-minute jog had left his calves burning and his back sore, but at least he'd tired out Run for the day.

After showering, he'd come to the café and plugged in the laptop Samantha had picked out for him. At the office, she'd also downloaded the TOR browser and installed the VPN and encrypted video app. It took him a while, but he figured out how to adjust the settings so the screen never went to sleep. Now, the computer sat on the chair next to him, open to the app. He didn't know what else to do except wait for a message he thought might never actually come.

Sy strolled in exactly on time wearing black slacks, a white button-up shirt, and sunglasses as black and shiny as her hair.

Austin stood as she walked in and took off the sunglasses. "You look too classy for this place."

"Please," she said, "sitting next to him. I may dress above my pay grade, but I'm a burger and beer kind of woman. And that's on a good day. I've been living off carrots and grocery store snacks for a week."

"I took the liberty of ordering you our new sandwich," Austin said. "You want coffee?"

She thought for a moment. "I'll take a half double-decaf macchiato with hemp milk, extra hot, light foam." She paused. "With a twist of lemon."

Austin stared at her.

"I'm joking, Austin. A black coffee, please."

He smiled, relieved. She had a good poker face.

Austin got her a cup of coffee, then sat back down. "So, this is awkward, but I have to come right out with it. I interviewed Bakes right before you."

"He told me you'd been there. I didn't think you and Rid and the others would drop the case just because we told you to."

"I also kind of overheard the call you made afterwards." He paused. "Overheard on purpose."

She gave him a stern look, then her face broke out in a sly smile. "You were eavesdropping on me? Like, hiding in the bushes or something?"

"Behind a tree," he admitted, staring at the table. "Not my finest moment. But when I get my teeth in a case, I..."

She waited until he looked up. "You go for it. I can understand that." She sipped her coffee. "I imagine you wanted to know—still want to know—why we boxed you out, boxed out the Sheriff's office."

Austin cocked his head. "I can't say it doesn't look shady."

"All I can say is, I was ordered to pull back from working with you fine people."

"Why?"

She smiled sarcastically. "What part of 'all I can say' was unclear?"

Austin tried another angle. "So why'd you begin working with us in the first place?"

"Standard practice. Big case. We had a lead, but why not let the locals help? Especially when it's Rid. That guy's one of the good ones."

"He is," Austin agreed. "So are you ready to tell me who asked you to involve me in the first place?" He already knew who it was, but what he didn't know was *why*.

Andy emerged from the kitchen and set down two waffle breakfast sandwiches. Austin said, "It's called the *I'm Too Cool for a Fork*."

"You are literally clueless," Andy said, shaking his head. "It's the *I'm Too Sleepy For My Fork*."

"*Right Said Fred*," Sy said. "I used to dance to that in college." She picked up the sandwich, which was bigger than both of her hands. "Looks amazing."

She took a huge bite, and they both ate in silence for a while. When she seemed to be taking a break, Austin said, "You have a suspect you like on the Foulweather Bluff murders?"

"Hey, buy a girl a drink first, will ya?"

Austin chuckled, gestured at her coffee. "I did, and a sandwich."

"Oh. Right. Yeah, we're close. Looking for someone." She eyed him. "You? Since I boxed Ridley out, he won't share much."

"No comment," Austin said. There was no way he was going to share what they'd found about Davey Wragg until he knew what Sy was up to, and he doubted that would happen anytime soon. "It seems as though you're not gonna tell me much more than I already know, so why did you want to have breakfast with me?"

She thought for a moment. "Since you eavesdropped on my

conversation, I imagine you heard the part when I said you were good looking. Plus, I asked you out to *dinner*, actually."

Austin frowned. "Do you enjoy being coy?"

"Sort of, yeah. Look, I asked you to dinner because Ridley said you were single and you seem like an interesting guy. My therapist said I should start dating again, if you want to know the truth. I promised her I'd ask one guy out in the next three months. That was four months ago."

"I'm, uhhh, flattered?"

She picked up the sandwich, studied it as though she might take another bite, then set it back down and took a sip of water. "Peace offering, okay?"

Austin was confused. "Huh?"

"I'll tell you who told me to ask for you specifically. Although you may not like it."

"Captain Luke Seymour Garrison."

She was surprised. "How'd you know?"

"Spoke with my mom. She said she used to know him."

"Wait, so you *know*?"

Now Austin was even more confused. "Know that my mom knows him, or knew him? Yeah."

Sy leaned back, looked down. Under normal circumstances, he would have thought she was hiding something, but she'd been hiding many things since the moment they met. This was something else. Embarrassment? Guilt?

"Sy, what is it?"

She looked up. "So you know that your mom knew Captain Garrison back in the day?"

"Sure, she said he had a thing for her. But, I mean, she was married and—"

Sy looked away again, clearly embarrassed. "*Happily* married?"

"What?" Austin asked. "You're saying..."

She reached across the table suddenly and squeezed his hand. "I'm sorry. I have no idea why I'm in the middle of this. Garrison told me he and your mom were more than friends. I think—and you know I'm telling the truth because my face is turning red as a candied apple—I think he asked me to involve you so he'd have an excuse to get back in touch with your mom."

Austin tasted bland citrus, like biting into a flavorless, desiccated orange. It was a childlike disappointment, like when he'd learned Santa Claus wasn't real. He pulled his hand away. "He told you he had an *affair* with my mom?"

She nodded. "I'm sorry. I... I mean I can't be sure he was telling the truth but..."

"But why would he lie?"

Sy frowned. "I feel like hell for being the one to tell you that." She slid her coffee cup back and forth across the wooden table. "He told me because he wanted to make sure I didn't think he was involved in the various shenanigans the Navy is up to around this case, around Vellory."

Austin had a technique he'd developed in the early days after the shooting that had killed Fiona and left him in the hospital. It was as though he'd developed a section of his brain where he could stuff information and close it off, not allowing it to seep into his consciousness. Often in those early days—and quite a few times since—he'd crammed his knowledge that Fiona was gone there just so he could get through a task, like driving a car or eating a meal. In this moment, he shoved in everything Sy had told him about his mom. He'd have to deal with it, but now wasn't the time.

"Can we change the subject?" he asked.

"Please. Anything else."

"Tell me straight. What do you know about Vellory? Sure seemed like you were covering for him—maybe because someone told you to—but from the stuff that's coming out in the papers, it seems like he's going down."

Sy said, "First of all, I wouldn't be so sure he's going down. Second of all, the news that's coming out about him..." She paused, making sure no one was within earshot. "It's all true. He was crooked as hell back in the day. That's off the record, by the way."

"I'm not a reporter, and there is no record."

She offered a wry smile. "I heard you might be dating a reporter."

Austin folded his arms. "I'm not." Frowning, he asked, "How are you going to tell your therapist our date is going?"

She laughed, rocking back in her chair. "You ever find yourself in a situation so absurd you can't believe it's real, then you snap your fingers and are like, 'This *is* real. This is *actually* happening.' That ever happen to you?"

Austin smiled. "Twice in the last half hour."

She laughed again, then settled back in and leaned forward. "There's a show I like called *30 Rock*. Heard of it?"

Austin shook his head.

"There's an episode where the main character is on a first date with a good looking guy and everything goes wrong. She finds out he has a kid, he sees her on the toilet by accident, his mom dies. All on their *first* date. And by the end, they're like, 'Well, if we make it through all this on day one and we still like each other, maybe we can make it through anything together."

Austin had to admit that, despite everything, he was interested in her in a way he hadn't been in anyone since Fiona. She'd acted shady, but something in him thought it was for a good reason, even though he didn't yet understand what that reason was. He knew that not everyone in law enforcement was in it for the right reasons, but he thought she was.

He'd been trying to deny it since meeting her, but something stirred in him when he was around her that he'd thought was gone. Something chaotic, inexplicable. In fact, he realized, that's why he'd been willing to eavesdrop on her conversation at the lake. It wasn't only to find out what she was up to. There was something about her that had made him irrational, reckless.

He stared at her as she sipped her coffee. And he was about to admit that he was interested, was about to ask her out on a real date. But instead, he heard himself saying, "I can't get past Vellory. I need to know you weren't covering for him."

She sighed. "I *was* covering for Vellory a bit, but not for the reasons you think." She stood. "Look, Austin, I can't say everything, but I'll tell you this. Sometime today, Ridley is going to get a call from some Navy lawyers. They'll be inviting him to a meeting. I'll be there, Vellory will be there." She polished off the last sip of coffee in her mug, and set it down on the table with a heavy thud. "I suggest you try to wrangle up an invitation. You won't want to miss it."

As she walked out, Austin glanced down at his new laptop, still open to the video messaging app. As it had been for the last hour, the video box was black.

CHAPTER TWENTY-TWO

AUSTIN PULLED into the alley behind Open Sea Sports Bar and Grille five minutes early, but from the look of it he was the last to arrive.

Sy had been right. About an hour after their breakfast ended, Austin got a call from Lucy, telling him to come in the back door of the sports bar in Silverdale at 2 PM that day. She didn't know why, but Vellory and his team of lawyers had requested a meeting with everyone involved in the investigation.

Four cars were parked along the fence in the alley, leaving just enough room for Austin to squeeze his truck through and take a spot at the end.

He smelled fry oil and onion rings, but it wasn't his synesthesia. The sports bar had a giant stainless steel exhaust fan shooting oily steam into the alley. He found the back door, which was propped open a crack with a little rubber wedge, and entered. A man in an expensive brown suit greeted him and ushered him into a banquet room at the back of the restaurant, then closed the door behind them.

Eight or ten people sat around a large circular table. Straight ahead was Vellory, flanked by two men on each side. Lawyers, from the look of them.

On the other side of the table, Ridley sat between Lucy and Jimmy. Sy stood along the wall, clearly there to observe, rather than participate.

Ridley said, "Austin is the last member of our team. Can you tell us what this is about?"

The man in the brown suit offered Austin a chair next to Jimmy, then walked over and stood next to Sy.

The lawyer on Vellory's right spoke first. "I'm Gregory Delaney, and I represent Mr. Vellory. I'm his personal lawyer. We don't need to go through a whole round of introductions, but the men to my right and left are Naval lawyers. You know Sy, and that's a member of her team from NCIS."

"What's this about?" Ridley asked. "We have an investigation to run."

"If you don't mind," Delaney said, his tone bitter and tight. He wore a dark blue suit and had a drooping left eye that twitched every third or fourth word. "You've been harassing my client for days, both in person and through scurrilous leaks in the press. We will do the talking."

Ridley leaned back. "Fine. Let's get on with it."

Delaney reached under the table and pulled out a small black backpack, from which he pulled a tape recorder that looked like it belonged in the 1990s. It was gray, about the size of a small Walkman, the kind of recorder Austin had used before everything went digital in the early 2000s.

Austin watched Vellory's pale blue eyes move from the recorder to his own. He squinted, not smiling but not frowning. For a man who was getting destroyed in the press, he seemed largely unconcerned.

Delaney picked up the recorder, his eye twitching even faster now. "On Memorial Day of 1992, my client met with Jack

Hammeron and Joey Blake after he left the bar that was, at the time, known as the Watering Hole. He recorded what occurred on the beach that night. As you're aware, vicious lies are being reported in the press these days about my client's actions during Operation Desert Storm." He cleared his throat. "Now, though Mr. Vellory has chosen not to speak on this publicly, yet, he is prepared to admit only in this room that some small indiscretions *did* occur."

Small indiscretions? Austin thought. The amount of evidence against Vellory that was leaking online was growing by the day. It was fairly clear that Vellory was guilty as hell, and the mountain of evidence was going to be too much to ignore. One way or another, he was going down, so Austin had to interpret everything out of this lawyer's mouth as nothing more than an attempt to squeeze out of any involvement his client had in the homicide.

"On that fateful night in 1992," Delaney continued, "my client met with Hammeron and Blake at Foulweather Bluff. Now, though we would rather not speak ill of the dead, both Blake and Hammeron had engaged in illegal actions in Iraq. My client intended to convince them to come clean."

"Wait wait wait," Ridley said, unable to contain himself. Austin had been watching his temples pop, his jaw tighten. He was as annoyed by this smarmy, BS'ing lawyer as Austin was. "I didn't come here to listen to your fairy tales. If there's something exculpatory on those tapes, hit play. Otherwise..." he glanced at Lucy and Jimmy... "we're leaving."

Delaney's eye stopped twitching and he glared across at Ridley. "The evidence *is* exculpatory. I want your word, Detective. When you hear it, if you agree, you will cease any murder investigation into my client and release a statement clearing him."

Ridley glared right back. He parted his gritted teeth to speak. "If that tape clears him of murder, I'll say it. All the other stuff—the fraud, the bribery..." He waved a hand dismissively. "Not my department."

"Of course," Delaney said. "We're dealing with those falsehoods separately."

"Then let's hear it," Ridley said. "And we'll want copies of the tape."

Delaney laughed. "We will be playing it once and only once. No copies will be provided."

Ridley looked down. Austin could tell he wanted to keep arguing, but they were in a position of weakness. Delaney and everyone else in the room knew just how desperate they were to hear what was on the tape.

"Do we have an agreement?" Delaney asked.

Ridley nodded.

Delany slid the recorder to the center of the table, finger poised above the play button. "It's faint," he said, his eye twitching. "I suggest you lean in to hear."

CHAPTER TWENTY-THREE

THE FIRST THING Austin heard was the whistling wind. He closed his eyes, picturing himself on the beach at Foulweather Bluff, an eerie feeling seeping through him. He could almost feel the cool air, see the dark branches waving in the night.

He heard breathing. Breathing from thirty years ago.

It was like he was going back in time.

He didn't trust Vellory or his lawyer, but he believed the tape was real. Vellory would have no reason to gather them together if he didn't think he had real evidence that could clear him of the murders.

Delaney paused the recording. "The breathing you hear is Mr. Vellory walking to the spot on the beach where he met Hammeron and Blake. The first voice you hear will be my client, followed by Hammeron with a deep voice and Blake with a lighter tone."

He started the recording again.

A few more seconds of wind and breathing, then Vellory's voice emerged from the recorder. "Boys, good to see you."

"Captain, glad you wanted to meet." Hammeron's deep voice cut through the whistling wind.

Then the mousey voice of Joey Blake, the youngest of the three. "Why are we all the way out here?"

Austin kept his eyes closed, picturing the three men standing on the beach. He heard their exchange almost like he was watching a play in his head.

Vellory: "I'll explain. Where's Del Guado?"

Hammeron: "He said he'd meet us here. Wife was hounding him about something and he had to stay back to call her from the bar. He should be here soon."

Blake: "Should we wait for him?"

Vellory: "I don't have much time. If I can get you both to see it my way, you can convince him. He'll listen to you."

Hammeron: "He will. We want to do the right thing."

Vellory: "Blake, what about you, do you want to do the right thing?"

Blake: "I'll do whatever Hammer says. He's been my man on this from the beginning, and I trust him."

Vellory: "Look, we're all gonna be okay on this thing. Trust me. I—"

Vellory broke off suddenly. Austin had thought he'd heard a faint pop, like a tree branch breaking.

Delaney paused the recording. "I don't know if you heard it, but that pop was a gunshot. My client stopped speaking because he heard a gunshot, a fact backed up by the other two men, which you'll hear in a moment."

He pressed play again.

Hammeron: "What was that?"

Blake: "Down the beach."

Vellory: "Is that?"

Another gunshot, this one closer and impossible to mistake. But it was an odd gunshot. Austin couldn't quite describe it, but it wasn't like any gun he'd ever fired. The Russian pistol, he thought.

Then another voice, or was it wind, or...

It sounded like someone calling, "Aaaaddeeeeeeeee."

Then another shot.

Next, footsteps and Vellory's heavy breaths.

Then Hammeron's voice: "Where are you going? It's Adam and..." His voice became inaudible as Vellory's breaths grew heavier and heavier.

Then gunshots. One, then two, then three. These ones sounded more familiar, more like a rifle.

Austin heard running footfalls over crackling branches and leaves as Vellory's breaths grew closer together, almost frantic. Then the tape went silent.

Delaney stopped the recording. The room was quiet.

Vellory's face looked genuinely pained. Lucy and Jimmy looked stunned. Ridley stared at Delaney.

Even Delaney appeared shaken. "My client met with Hammeron and Blake. He had planned to meet with Adam Del Guado and—"

"Let me tell it," Vellory interrupted. "My men deserve that."

One of the gray-suited lawyers leaned over and whispered something in his ear, but he shook him off. "I know how to speak without incriminating myself," Vellory barked.

Vellory looked at Austin, then Ridley. "Del Guado came running down the beach. Someone was chasing him. God as my witness I don't know who. Tall guy, lean, that's all I know. He shot Adam in the back, and I ran. Hammer rushed to help Del Guado. That man would have run into a burning building to fight Satan just to save a kitten." He shook his head, as though awed by Hammer's memory. "Blake—smart as hell, but always followed Hammer—joined him. I'm not proud of running. I didn't know what was going on, and I didn't look back once. I can only assume they were both shot. I didn't see them fall, but in my head, in my heart, I knew." His lips quivered. "The fallen of Foulweather Bluff."

After a long silence, Lucy said, "Why'd you lie about the time you left the bar?"

"Don't answer that," Delaney said.

Vellory kicked back his chair and stood, glaring at Lucy, but his voice was as practiced and calm as ever. "I left at eight, went home, got the recorder, then went back to meet them at the beach at ten." He cleared his throat and looked at his lawyers. "That's enough of this." Then, he locked eyes with Austin. "I hope you'll stop bothering me now and go find the man who killed those boys."

The lawyers all stood. Ridley and the others stood.

As Vellory and his team packed away the recording and left, Austin had a hundred questions. Why had Vellory recorded the conversation? Had he heard anything else from Del Guado, anything the tape didn't catch? Was there anything else he could say about the man who'd shot Del Guado? What had the first couple gunshots sounded like to him?

Austin had also heard an odd break in the recording, as though a section had been cut out from the initial conversation between Vellory, Hammer, and Blake. But he wasn't sure about that and knew it would do no good to ask.

But the main thing running through Austin's mind was that it appeared as though Vellory was telling the truth about what happened that night. At least, some of the truth. Clearly, someone else had been on the beach, someone else had killed the three men.

Everything he'd heard on the recording matched the lead they'd already been chasing. Davey Wragg was tall and lean. Apparently, he'd argued with both Del Guado and Hammer at different times. And the difference in the sounds of the gunshots fit the two types of bullet casings found near the bones.

As they walked out into the sun, Austin put it together in his mind. Somehow, Wragg had tailed Adam Del Guado to the beach and killed him with the rare Russian pistol. Maybe he'd always wanted to use it, but had brought the rifle just in case. And when Hammer and Blake charged, he'd used the other firearm.

After shooting Del Guado in the back, Wragg had killed his two buddies for the simple crime of rushing in to help.

CHAPTER TWENTY-FOUR

AUSTIN HAD HEARD something else on the recording, something that caught his attention for a reason he couldn't explain.

It was the voice, the call that was barely audible through the whistling wind. It had sounded like: *Aaaaddeeeeeeeee.*

There was something about it, but what?

He wanted to talk it over with Lucy and the others, but he didn't get the chance.

As he approached the parked cars outside the sports bar, he saw Sheriff Daniels leaning on Ridley's car, a sarcastic grin across his face that worried Austin more than his hardest scowl ever could have.

"Uh oh," Jimmy whispered. "He came back early."

Ridley, to his credit, said nothing at all. The sun was setting, casting a gorgeous, orange-pink glow across the alley, contrasting with the oily smell in the air and the nasty look on Daniels' face.

Daniels shoved his hands in his pockets as they approached. "Do you know where I'm supposed to be right now?"

They all nodded.

"And do you know why I came back from the Sheriff's

convention early?"

They nodded again.

Before he could continue, Ridley said, "Sheriff Daniels, this is on me. I ordered them to continue the investigation."

Daniels slowly looked from Jimmy to Lucy, from Lucy to Austin. "That true?"

No one admitted it, but no one denied it either. Ridley had made them all promise to let him take the fall.

"So," Daniels said, pacing in a small square. "You not only continued investigating a beloved Admiral—an Admiral with the nationwide popularity of—oh, I don't know—Dolly Parton, or The Rock. Hell, that guy is more beloved than all four Beatles combined in 1967. You not only investigated him when I ordered you not to, it turns out he's innocent? And don't get me started on how much damage that article did. Accident or no... well, someone has to fry for this."

Lucy had tried to bite her lip, but she couldn't hold back. "He might be innocent of the murders, sir, but he's far from innocent. And that popularity you're talking about, that was before news of his fraud and bribery broke."

Daniels scowled at her. "Stay out of this."

"Sir," Ridley said, "You didn't hear the tape in there. Even if he didn't fire the shots, he's been lying since the beginning. We were close."

"I didn't need to, you imbecile. When top Navy brass tells me they'll handle it, you know what I do. I say, 'Sir, yes sir.' Which is what you said to me before going behind my back!" Daniels shook his head, then turned at Lucy. "You're young, but your record is good. With the way things are going, it would look good for my governor campaign in a few years if I have a woman as lead detective."

Lucy eyed him suspiciously, holding a hand up to her forehead, shielding her pale, freckled face from the sun. "Sheriff, I would never—"

"You don't have a choice," Daniels said. He jabbed a thumb at Ridley. "Three months unpaid leave. And a write up. Take it, or resign. Final offer." He turned back to Lucy. "You're now my lead detective. Don't screw it up."

Austin was too stunned to say anything. Jimmy looked from Ridley to Lucy.

Ridley stood, silent as a statue, hands in his pockets. It appeared as though he was going to back off, live to fight another day.

"We good?" Daniels asked.

"No," Lucy said, suddenly. "I have a condition."

"You're not in any position to—"

"Two conditions, actually. Or I quit, along with Jimmy."

Jimmy nodded.

"And me," Austin added.

Lucy and Daniels stared each other down for a long moment, then Daniels shrugged.

"First, don't ever call Ridley an imbecile again. He's either Ridley or Black Sherlock, and he's the best detective any of us know. Second, we're one hundred percent free to finish investigating this case. Without interference."

Daniels smirked, as though all of this was exactly as he'd expected.

He was quiet a long time, then a change came over him and he let out a long sigh. "My sponsor says I need to learn to apologize more freely." He turned to Ridley. "I'm sorry I said that. I know you're good at your job, except when it comes to the politics." Then he grew angry again. "I'm *not* sorry about any of the other stuff. You really screwed me, screwed yourself. But I shouldn't have said that." Then, back to Lucy. "Investigate away. Now that Vellory is cleared of the murders, we need to find the real killers ASAP. For the fraud and whatnot, he will get his comeuppance, both in the press and from the Navy. But as far as the murder, the sooner you solve it, the better."

As Daniels drove away, the four of them stood in the alley.

It was Ridley who spoke first. "I've been wanting to spend more time with Rachel anyway."

His tone was deadpan, but Austin saw a slight twinkle in his eye.

Jimmy chuckled. "Glad you can find the positive in this. You really have turned philosophical."

Lucy said, "If me and Austin hadn't given those quotes to Anna, if her editor hadn't..."

"Woulda coulda shoulda," Ridley said. "Three months off ain't so bad. Before I go, there was something on that tape, something in the shout." He scrunched up his forehead, thinking.

"I thought so, too," Austin said.

Ridley shook his head. "Could you tell if it was Wragg's voice?"

"Wish I could have," Austin replied, "but the tape is thirty years old, and the wind, and..."

Ridley nodded. "Yeah. Look, the wire is up on Wragg's mother." He smiled. "When Daniels hears what I had to do to get that wiretap so quickly..." He turned to Lucy. "Well, don't assume my suspension will actually end in three months." Lucy tried to object, but Ridley steamrolled over her. "Samantha is our go-between with the East Seattle police on that."

He paused, like he might keep going on the specifics of the case, then his face filled with emotion. "Lucy, you have all my confidence."

He looked from Austin to Jimmy. "All my confidence."

He patted Lucy on the shoulder, then squeezed his massive frame into the driver's seat of his car and eased out of the alley, leaving the three of them in silence.

"What the hell is happening?" Jimmy asked.

Lucy said, "I think this is one of those times when the kid looks up from a mess they've made and realizes their daddy is no longer there to help them. We're on our own."

"You got this, Lucy," Jimmy said.

Lucy frowned. "No nickname?"

"Yeah," Austin said. "You could have gone with Lucy O'Leader, Lucy O'Luminary, Lucy O'... well, I can't think of any more. But I'm sure you could have thought of something."

Jimmy wasn't smiling, and Austin thought he knew what he was thinking. Having your fiance become your boss was a lot to take in.

Lucy said, "I hereby order you to call me a bunch of stupid nicknames."

Jimmy smiled. "Ma'am, yes ma'am, Lucy O'Lawgiver."

Lucy punched his arm. "You can do better than that."

Jimmy thought. "Lucy O'Leprechaun? Oh, I got it: Lucy O'Loooooser."

"Loser?" she asked, unimpressed.

Austin tuned out their playful banter.

He couldn't stop playing the recording over and over in his mind. The fact that something had stuck with Ridley as well confirmed his suspicion, but he wasn't getting any closer. And he knew there was no way to get a copy of the recording. Vellory's army of lawyers would make sure of that.

Austin said, "Sorry to interrupt, but what are our next moves?"

Lucy said, "To me, it all comes down to Wragg. Vellory is obviously guilty of various things, but he didn't kill those guys. We find Wragg, this whole thing breaks open. But how the hell do we find him, other than hoping he calls his mom?"

"We don't have to rely on hope for that," Austin said.

"What do you mean?" Jimmy asked.

Austin smiled. "You ever heard of tickling the wires?"

CHAPTER TWENTY-FIVE

SY WAS ONLY a mile from home, ready to get in the tub with a glass of red wine, when her phone rang. She'd told herself she wouldn't take any more calls today. After the week she'd had, she *needed* the night off. But she couldn't keep herself from glancing at the caller-ID.

It was Benny Ramirez. Again.

He'd begged her to come to the meeting with Vellory and even though she'd shot him down, she'd known he'd try to find out what happened soon after it ended.

Reluctantly, she answered. "What, Benny?"

"You said only to call you with something urgent. Well, I have something urgent."

For Benny, every single development was urgent. He'd once called her at 9PM on a Saturday to tell her that some DNA had come back from the lab, even though the report only stated that the results had been inconclusive.

In her head, she sometimes called him *It-Could-Have-Waited-'Til-Monday* Ramirez. Still, better to be overly cautious than lackadaisical.

Benny said, "I assume the meeting went well. Vellory is in the clear, on the murders, at least. Right?"

Sy took a sharp right turn up a hill that led to her apartment building. She could almost taste the wine now. "*That's* what was urgent?"

He laughed nervously. "Um, no. Sorry. List of assets that could be tied to Michael Wragg. Just emailed them to you."

"Any other residences, phones, anything that will help us find him?"

"Not as such."

"Not *as such*? What the hell does that mean?" Sy had a rule never to take work home with her. Even if it meant being gone twelve hours a day, her apartment was her sanctuary. She'd either check this email now, or it would wait until tomorrow. She pulled over into the lot of another apartment building.

"It means no," Benny said, "with a *but*."

"And the 'but' is?"

"Wragg's father, when he died, owned a tiny gravel company up on Graystone Mountain in West Bremerton. It didn't pass to his son, but it's been tied up legally for a decade. It doesn't belong to Wragg, but it doesn't *not* belong to him either."

She opened the email he'd sent, clicked the attachment, and scrolled down. "Interesting. Says here it's twenty acres, and includes a concrete utility building."

"Figured they used that to power their equipment."

"Any idea what's actually going on there now?" Sy asked.

"Googled it and there's nothing. I think kids might go there to drink beer and make out."

Sy pictured the bottle of wine on her counter. It would still be there in an hour. She tapped the address into the map screen on her dashboard. "I'm fifteen minutes away. Where are you?"

"At home, I'll be there in ten."

"Stay at least a hundred yards back from any structure. Wait for me to arrive."

"Got it."

"And Benny, good job. That's a good find. We bring this bastard in, you'll be in my job before you know it."

"Thanks." Benny hung up.

He'd only gotten out of the office once or twice so far in his career, and Sy could see him bolting for the door like a puppy heading to the park.

She pulled out into traffic, made a u-turn, and headed west.

Graystone Mountain wasn't much of a mountain. Sy's grandmother lived only fifty miles from Mount Fuji in Japan. Now, *that* was a mountain. Its size and beauty dominated the landscape, making you aware of it at all times while in its presence.

Graystone Mountain, on the other hand, was a glorified hill, no more than 2,000 feet high and mostly owned by logging and quarrying companies. Still, it was pretty enough from a distance, and was said to have some decent trails on the north side, which was owned by the city.

The road leading up it turned from gravel to dirt about a thousand feet up, and Sy took the turn marked with an ancient, rusted sign: *Wragg's Gravel*. She turned on her high beams, navigating a mile or two of twistbacks and sharp curves and never topping twenty miles an hour.

Finally, she came to a clearing. Ahead, a pit in the mountain appeared to have once been a quarry. She assumed that, like most abandoned quarries, it was half-full of water, on top of which a few ducks nibbled at garbage, probably tossed in by local teenagers.

She cursed when she saw Benny's Toyota, which was parked closer than she'd advised, more like twenty yards from the utility building. Always the eager beaver.

As she parked beside him, she was surprised when he didn't look over. He appeared to be staring straight ahead. Sy followed the direction of his gaze to the entrance to the utility building. Nothing. The building, lit by her headlights, was a dense square of cement roughly ten by ten feet, with thick wires extending from the top and disappearing into the woods.

She got out and walked around to the front of his car. Her breath caught in her throat. There was broken glass on his hood.

Then she saw the blood.

She covered her mouth.

Benny's front window had been shot out. And Benny himself had been shot through the head.

He was dead.

She swiveled, reaching for her phone, but it was too late.

"Raise your hands, women. Don't reach for that phone." A man had stepped out of the utility building. Michael Wragg. His rifle was aimed at her chest and, according to his record, he'd once been a Navy Seal, which meant he knew how to use it.

Sy raised her hands slowly. "Wragg. It's not too late to do the right thing. I—"

"Quiet. I usually like a mouthy women, but I just killed a man, and nothing gets me off like that. Not even a piece like you."

Sy's insides recoiled. She cursed herself for putting Benny in that position, for putting herself in this position.

Wragg stepped toward her and gestured toward the utility shed. "Come here. And be quick about it."

CHAPTER TWENTY-SIX

AUSTIN FLOPPED ONTO THE COUCH, exhausted. He'd had some long days in the NYPD, but something about this one had left him tired in a way he hadn't felt for years.

Still, he found the energy to open the laptop sitting on his coffee table. The video messaging app was open. No missed calls.

Run finished the dinner he'd put in her bowl when he got home, and bounded into the living room holding a tennis ball in her mouth. Austin picked it up wearily and tossed it into the kitchen, then closed his eyes. Seconds later, she was back, barking politely to alert him to the fact that she had returned and it was time for another throw.

Grabbing the ball, he heard a strange beep. Somewhere between a *ding* and a *wind chime*. Suddenly, the video app lit up: *Incoming Call.*

Scrambling, he clicked the *Accept Call* button, then clicked to make the app full screen. Almost instantly, a man appeared. Austin adjusted the laptop so his face was in front of the little camera at the top of the screen, as Samantha had shown him.

"Hello," he said. "Who's there? How did you know I was home?"

"Hold on," the man said. He was leaning in toward the camera like he was trying to get a better look at Austin. But after a moment Austin realized that he was studying something on his screen.

Despite being in a fairly dark room, the man wore sunglasses along with a blank baseball hat low on his forehead. A bandana covered his nose and mouth. In fact, the only parts of his face that Austin could see were his ears, eyes, and an inch or so of his jaw line. Clearly, he didn't want Austin to be able to identify him.

Finally, the man spoke again, leaning back. "Okay. I was checking the network. We're alone. The way I knew you were home was that I hacked your computer this morning. I can tell when it's on and off." He paused. "I'm Michael Lee, and you've been looking for me."

Austin didn't know what to say. A thousand questions had been burning inside him ever since he realized that Lee could be a real person, not a fictional character in Fiona's planned novel. The detective in him knew he should start slow, start at the beginning. He should try to get all the details on the way up to the big picture.

But in that moment, the thoughtful detective inside Austin took a back seat to the grieving husband. "Did you know Fiona Austin? And do you know what happened to her?"

Lee shook his head. "I have never heard of her."

Austin's insides twisted. He had known it wouldn't be that easy, but knowing something won't happen doesn't always crowd out the hope that it will.

He took a deep breath and went back to the beginning. "Are you the Michael Lee who met a woman named Megan at Mama Dae's Korean BBQ?"

"Yes."

"You met Megan on a dating app?"

"Yes."

"Please," Austin said, "tell me what happened next."

Lee's voice was monotone, as though he was describing what happened to someone else, someone he didn't care about. "I had been on the app for a year with little interest. Few connections. Megan and I hit it off right away. All the same interests. She liked my David Bowie t-shirt. At least she said so." He paused, shaking his head.

Austin had once worked on a case that began similarly. A man posing as a woman would connect with married men on dating apps—always sharing all the same interests and hobbies—then try to extort money from them after getting them to send compromising messages or photos. Catfishing, he'd heard it called.

"So we met for dinner," Lee continued, "and afterwards we were going to go back to her place. East Village. I was excited because this kind of thing doesn't happen to me much. I should have known better."

"What happened next?" Austin asked.

"Taxi let us out and we were at her door. At least, I thought it was her door." He paused, as though composing himself, then continued. "I started getting a funny feeling. She was looking around as she opened the door, like she was expecting someone. A big SUV pulled up, and I ran. Luckily, I was already a little paranoid. Three men chased me down the alley. They were big and slow. I'm little and fast. I got away."

"Okay," Austin said. It wasn't much, but it matched Fiona's story, the little of it he had. But from the way Lee had described it, either he was simply paranoid, or he'd had a good reason to be on guard. And Austin thought he might know why. "Are you an informant?"

"Yes."

"You were, and are, offering evidence against the Namgung crime family?"

Lee adjusted his hat, pulling it down even lower on his forehead. "Yes."

"Who are you working with?"

"The FBI."

"And you don't know anything about a DA named Fiona Austin? You don't know if she was looking into the Namgung family, the NYPD, or even elements of the FBI?"

Lee shook his head. "I was hoping you could tell me more."

This took Austin by surprise. "What would *I* be able to tell *you?*"

Lee paused, leaning in again as though studying his screen. "I only have a minute or two. The Feds are trying to access my system. Make sure I'm keeping to myself."

"What? What does that mean?"

"I'm not supposed to be speaking with anyone."

That led right into Austin's next line of thinking. "If my call almost got you killed, why did you contact me?"

"You're a former cop, I thought you might be able to help me."

"Help you what?"

"Get me out of my current situation. I'm working with the FBI, but they're as corrupt as the people I'm informing on. This whole thing is a spider web of corruption. I'm just a fly caught in the middle of their web."

Austin felt sick. He recalled the warning of John Johnson, who'd told him that the NYPD itself had corrupt elements dealing narcotics to and from Southeast Asia. There were a hundred possibilities, but it was quite possible Fiona had been investigating elements of the NYPD, possibly working together with the FBI. And since Austin worked in the NYPD, that would explain why she'd never mentioned the investigation to him.

Lee continued, "I want to know if there's anyone I can speak with in the NYPD. Anyone a hundred percent trustworthy."

Without thinking, Austin blurted, "DMJ. David Min-Jun.

He's one of my closest friends in the NYPD and you can trust him. But what are you hoping he can do?"

"Help me escape."

Austin couldn't even think through all the ramifications of it. "I can give you his number."

For the first time, Lee pulled down his bandana, exposing a face that hadn't seen the sun in a long time. His upper lip had been gashed towards his cheek and sown back together. The two-inch scar pulled his expressions leftward giving him an odd, crooked smile.

But it *was* a smile. "David Min-Jun. Got it. I won't need any help finding him."

Lee leaned forward, reaching for his keyboard, and Austin's screen went black.

CHAPTER TWENTY-SEVEN

AUSTIN HAD BEEN WAITING in the conference room for an hour when Lucy and Jimmy walked in. They'd been over in East Seattle, tickling the wires.

It was a technique he and his partners had often used back in New York. When looking for a suspect who was in hiding, sometimes they would wiretap people close to the suspect—family, friends, business associates—then interview those people in hopes that one of them would get sloppy and contact the person they were actually trying to locate.

It rarely worked on experienced criminals, but worked well on those who hadn't thought things through. He only hoped that Wragg and his mother fell into the second camp.

"How'd it go?" Austin asked as they sat across from him.

"Davey Wragg's mother was an odd duck," Jimmy said. "Sweet one minute, angry the next. I'm not one to diagnose someone out of the blue, but she definitely came off as a little nutso."

Lucy kicked her feet up on the table. "*Nutso* isn't a diagnosis, Jimmy. Besides, she was *faking* it. I think she knows exactly where he is, or at least how to get in touch with him." She turned to Austin. "Anyway, we did what you suggested. Didn't come right out and accuse him of anything, but came close. Any concerned mother would call her son immediately. She denied having a number for him, but I think she does."

Jimmy said, "All she knew was that he lived somewhere in Hansville. Claimed she didn't even have an address. And I believed her. I think she was more crazy than deceitful."

"We have a bet going," Lucy said. "If she calls her son in the next twenty-four hours, we honeymoon in Europe."

"And if she doesn't," Jimmy interjected, "we honeymoon in Hawaii."

Austin looked around the room. "Am I still the only one who knows you two are engaged."

"Thanks for keeping it quiet," Jimmy said, nodding. "It was complicated before. With Lucy as my boss, well, now's not the time to visit the HR department, which we don't have local access to anyway."

Samantha came in, only carrying a single laptop. "It's not the same without Ridley, is it?"

Lucy frowned, "It's really not."

Jimmy turned to Lucy, "Hey, Lucy O-Leadership-Qualities, shouldn't you be standing in the front of the room, tapping on the whiteboard with a marker?"

She frowned. "Those are Ridley's markers."

He shook his head, feigning deep disappointment. "Lucy O'Not-Ready-To-Lead."

She tossed a pen at his head, which he dodged. "I'm ready, just not ready to use his markers. Plus, we've got nothing to write."

"Actually, you do," Samantha said, opening her laptop. "Just got off the phone with the Seattle PD. They're emailing me a call Wragg's mother made ten minutes ago." She studied the screen. "Yup, just arrived."

Austin wasn't surprised that Lucy's read on the situation had been correct. "Let's hear it," he said.

Samantha turned the laptop to face them and pressed play as everyone leaned in to hear.

Davey Wragg: Mom?

Mrs. Wragg: How'd you know it was me?

Davey Wragg: Caller-ID.

Mrs. Wragg: You said to call this number if anyone came by. They came by. Detectives. What the hell did you do this time?

Davey Wragg: Nothin', Ma. I didn't do nothin'.

Mrs. Wragg: Then why are they asking questions?

Davey Wragg: Police harassment.

Mrs. Wragg: Something about some Navy boys.

Davey Wragg: I didn't do nothin'.

Mrs. Wragg: And I *told* 'em that.

Davey Wragg: Mama?

Mrs. Wragg: Yeah, boy?

Davey Wragg: I can't go home no more.

Mrs. Wragg: Why?

Davey Wragg: They're looking for me there.

Mrs. Wragg: Come see me here.

Davey Wragg: Can't. They're looking for me there, too. Probably why they went to talk to you.

Mrs. Wragg: Where are you?

Davey Wragg: Mama, I'm... I'm scared.

Mrs. Wragg: Don't be a sissy, boy. Whatever you did, they probably had it coming.

Davey Wragg: I didn't do *nothin'*.

Mrs. Wragg: I know you didn't.

Davey Wragg: I... I have a women.

Mrs. Wragg: What?

Davey Wragg: I took a women.

Mrs. Wragg: A woman? Why the hell you can't tell the difference between *woman* and *women*, I'll never understand.

Davey Wragg: That's how pa said it.

Mrs. Wragg: Don't do anything bad, Davey.

Davey Wragg: Mama, I gotta go. Bye mama.

The call ended.

Lucy said, "What did he mean when he said he took a women?"

"He meant 'woman,'" Jimmy said.

"I know *that*," Lucy said, walking over to the whiteboard and picking up a marker. "But when? Do you think he has a hostage or... I mean he could have been talking about another crime, years ago." She sighed, setting down the marker.

"I don't know," Austin said. "But I know he gave us nothing we can use to locate him."

Lucy nodded. "We have his phone number now, but it'll take half a day, maybe twenty-four hours to get a warrant to force the cellphone company to tell us where he was at the time of the call." She paced. "And it sounds like he was worried about a wire. Not too worried to ignore the call, which was probably on a burner. But he didn't want to say where he was, which means he won't be there by the time we get a location from the phone company."

Samantha stood and walked around the conference table, using her index finger to trace the calligraphy tattoo that ran up her forearm. Austin had learned that this was one of her thinking ticks.

Lucy had, too. "What is it, Samantha? I can see that big brain working."

She stopped. Turned. "Just trying to figure out whether I'm willing to risk my career for this case."

Lucy stood. "What is it?"

Samantha said, "It won't hold up in court, and it's totally out of bounds. I—"

The door swung open suddenly and Daniels appeared in the doorway. "Has anyone heard from Sy? Symone Aoki?"

"Not since yesterday," Austin said. "At the meeting with Vellory."

"No one has seen her since," Daniels said, his voice full of concern. "She's missing. I told NCIS we'd double our efforts."

Austin tasted the dry burnt-toast bitterness that always came with dread. Wragg was in the wind, and now, so was Sy. It didn't take much of a leap for Austin to conclude that she'd been close to nabbing Wragg, then been taken. Or worse.

"Samantha," Lucy said, "get that recording to NCIS. Even if they're not going to help us, we have to help them." She turned to Daniels. "And boss, we've already doubled our efforts. Will they tell us where she was last seen, or—"

Daniels shook his head. "They won't share anything. They already know we're looking at Wragg. So are they. All I can say is, if you've already doubled your efforts, double them again." Daniels left, shutting the door behind him.

All eyes fell on Samantha, who offered a worried smile in Lucy's direction. "I can get a general vicinity of the location of the cell phone Wragg just used."

"What?" Lucy exclaimed. "Why didn't you tell us that from the jump?"

"Because," Samantha said, "it's completely illegal."

CHAPTER TWENTY-EIGHT

MINUTES LATER, Lucy and Austin were racing toward west Bremerton, heading for a place called Graystone Mountain. Austin had never heard of it, but Samantha had assured them that Wragg's cellphone had pinged off three different towers located on or around the mountain.

It turned out that Samantha was dating a guy she called a "white hat hacker." He'd studied computer science and coding at the University of Washington, but dropped out to work on a startup in Seattle. A year later, he'd cashed out, not wealthy, but financially comfortable for the rest of his life at age 23. He'd decided to use his skills for what he considered good causes. She hadn't told them much, but in this case he'd found a weakness in the system of the cellphone carriers that allowed him to search a phone number and figure out which cellphone towers it had recently connected to.

It was the same information they could get through a warrant, but it had been delivered in minutes, not hours or days.

Lucy took a sharp left, swerved across the center divide to pass a slow car, then veered back into her lane. Jimmy was behind them, though he had a hard time keeping up with Lucy's driving.

"Here's the thing I don't understand," Austin said. "It's about the Vellory meeting."

"Only *one* thing," Lucy said. "I've got a list."

Austin chuckled nervously as Lucy slowed only slightly, blasting through a red light. "Let's assume Vellory is telling the whole truth, which he isn't. Let's say he's innocent of the corruption and he wanted to meet with his men to convince them to come clean. Still, for thirty years he had evidence about their murders that he withheld. He lied to investigators at the time, and he lied to us."

Lucy turned up a steep hill, the road suddenly turning to gravel as they blasted past a sign listing multiple quarries and the name of a logging company.

"My bet," Lucy said, "is that he was the ringleader of all the corruption. I mean, he has to keep denying it, but the evidence is there. My thinking is that one or all of the men wanted to come clean, admit what they'd done, and he was trying to convince them to clam up. The recording sounded doctored to me, and maybe he cut that part out. Meanwhile, Wragg has had some argument with Del Guado at the bar. Wragg heads home, gets his guns, chases Del Guado down the beach and kills him. When he sees the other men, he takes them out as well. Witnesses. And Vellory—coward that he is—*runs*. While Hammer and Blake ran to help their friend, he bolted, left them to die to save his own ass."

"So then why admit it now? Why play us that recording?"

"He's going down for the corruption thing, but the Navy takes care of its own. It has an interest in protecting its reputation. So maybe he doesn't get any more TV deals, book deals. He's already rich. Who cares? But being under a cloud of suspicion for murder? That's too far."

Austin nodded along. "That *is* what his lawyer said. I just assumed everything out of his mouth was a lie, but I guess it's plausible."

They were right in the center of the triangle formed by the three cellphone towers Samantha's boyfriend had indicted. Austin saw the sign for Wragg's Gravel. "There!"

Lucy slammed on the breaks, backed up, and turned down the dirt road.

Two cars were parked out front, one of which was Sy's white SUV. Until that moment, part of him had hoped they'd been wrong, hoped she'd just been ignoring her phone, or had gotten sick and slept in.

Lucy stopped fifty yards back from the cars.

"Should we wait for Jimmy?" Austin asked.

"You have your weapon?"

"I do."

"I'll take the lead." As she got out of the car, she unholstered her firearm and pointed it toward the odd cement building near the cars. "Looks like a pretty good hideout."

Austin pulled out his gun and followed about a yard behind Lucy as she moved toward the building. In addition to Sy's car, a Toyota with a busted windshield was parked out front. It appeared to be empty, but the front seat was marked with blood.

About ten yards from the building, Lucy stopped. "Do you smell weed?"

Austin had smelled it at the same moment. "And I heard something."

"Laughter, or giggling?"

He gestured to the utility building with his gun. "From inside."

"Kitsap County police!" Lucy shouted. "Come out with your hands up."

The building had no windows. Only a large metal door.

As it began to move, Austin leveled his gun on it, aiming for the chest height of whatever figure was going to emerge from behind it.

With a grating metallic screech, the door slowly swung open, revealing two terrified teenagers, shivering in the soft morning light cutting through the trees.

The young man was shirtless and clothed only in boxer shorts. His hands were high in the air. Behind him, a teenaged girl stood in jeans and a bra, shielding her chest with one arm, the other raised above her head.

Austin's chest dropped. He lowered his gun.

The boy trembled. "We... um... we were just... just fooling around."

CHAPTER TWENTY-NINE

SY TWISTED HER WRISTS, trying to loosen the duct tape. It didn't give more than a millimeter or two. Although Wragg had made the mistake of binding her wrists with her hands in front of her, rather than behind her back, it wouldn't make much difference. She could move her fingers, but she couldn't stand, bound as she was to the metal radiator.

Wragg hadn't taken his eyes off her. Even in the middle of the night when she'd woken up, he'd been sitting by the window, gun on his lap, watching her.

"Was that your mother?" Sy asked again. She'd asked three times since Wragg had received the call, but he only ignored her. She just wanted to get him talking, to find a weakness that would allow her to create an opening.

"You said you were scared," she continued. "I can understand that, and I can help you."

Wragg paced back and forth along the cold floor, kicking empty plastic soda bottles and wrappers out of his way. She wasn't sure where she was, but she knew it wasn't far from the cement utility shed where he'd ambushed her. He'd said little, simply thrown a hood over her head and pushed her up what felt like a steep hill. They'd walked for five, maybe ten minutes, through crackling leaves and over branches. She'd fallen once or twice, but he'd yanked her up violently, repeating the same phrase over and over. "Get up, women."

When he'd pulled off the hood, the first thing she'd seen were antlers, four or five sets, mounted on the wall of what she assumed was a hunting cabin. It was odd, the things you think about while in captivity. She'd realized quickly that there was nothing she could do to escape, so she'd puzzled over his odd use of "woman" and "women," swapping the singular for the plural, and vice versa. It was a little quirk of speech that she might have found fascinating under different circumstances.

"I swear I can help you," she said. "There's an old saying. *Mizu ni nagasu.*"

"Don't speak no foreign language to me, women."

It wasn't much, but at least it was a reaction.

"I don't speak much Japanese," she said. "Lived here all my life. My grandma taught it to me. *Mizu ni nagasu.* It means, 'Let the water flow.' People sometimes translate it as, 'A river carries away bad memories,' or the more American: 'Water under the bridge.'"

She had his attention now. Her read on Wragg was that he was capable of extreme brutality. But also that he was unstable. Far from a criminal mastermind. Thirty years ago he'd killed three men and had been hiding out in Hansville ever since, not far from the scene of the crime. She knew he was capable of murder. He'd killed Benny the night before. But now he was stuck. He had nowhere left to run, probably little money and few friends. She needed to take advantage of the desperation she was sure he was feeling.

"So what?" he barked.

"It means that whatever you did in the past, it is in the past. It doesn't have to make you do anything now that you'll regret. I know you're a good person. You only did what you had to do." She wanted to shout, to call him names, all of which would only be second best to sticking him through the chest with a set of the sharp antlers hanging on the wall. But her instinct to stay alive had kicked in. It shamed her, but right now she would say anything she needed to say to stay alive.

"How did you find me? Are you at my house?"

"There are probably people there now, yes."

"Will they find us here?" He was trying to sound tough, even menacing, but his words betrayed the scared little boy inside. If she hadn't loathed him so much, she might have pitied him.

"I don't know where we are," she said. "So I can't know if they will find us."

"Up the hill half a mile. Hunting cabin belonged to my old men."

"Your old *man*?"

"We say *men*." His words came out with a spray of spittle.

"Why?"

"Just how we talk. No reason."

He seemed upset, and she decided not to press it.

After tying her to the radiator, he'd disappeared for half an hour, likely covering their trail up the mountain from the utility shed. "What did you do with Benny's body?"

"Who's Benny?" he asked.

She glared at him, unable to hide her disdain.

"Oh, right. They'll *never* find him."

"My people are good. They'll probably find us here." She didn't believe this. In the email Benny had sent, there had been no mention of a hunting cabin. Most likely it had been built without a permit and never made it onto the county records. "But my car is down there. Half a tank of gas. And my purse. You could have a thousand dollars and a car ten minutes from now." She liked her chances better if they were on the move.

"My car is parked nearby."

"But they won't be looking for mine like they'll be looking for yours."

He considered this. "If I go, I'm taking you."

She smiled, not seductively—she couldn't manage that, even if she believed it would help her—but kindly. "It's your best bet. I suggest you leave now, though. They could be here soon."

Anywhere was better than here.

CHAPTER THIRTY

WHILE LUCY QUESTIONED the teenagers out by the cars, Austin and Jimmy inspected the utility shed. The smell of marijuana was strong, but it was clear that the teenagers weren't the only ones who'd been there.

Austin used the tip of a pen to pick up a roll of silver duct tape. He shined his cellphone light on it, examining the edges, which were fairly bright. "Jimmy, you see this?"

Jimmy examined it. "What?"

"See how the frayed edges, the little white strings on the adhesive side are bright? That means it's been used recently. They darken over time."

Jimmy leaned in, then shook his head. "If you say so."

"And the cigarettes," Austin said. "Get the ash tray and bring it out. Use gloves, or slide it onto something without touching it."

A moment later, Jimmy joined him out in the light. Together they approached the teenagers, whose alarm level had dropped from sheer terror to embarrassed nervousness. They'd put their clothes on, jeans and matching Bremerton High School sweatshirts, which actually made them a pretty cute couple, given the circumstances.

Austin asked the girl, "The cigarettes, they yours?"

She shook her head, causing a cascade of brown hair to fall in front of her eyes as a hair tie popped loose. She brushed it away. "Cigarettes? No way. Never. Kids chill here sometimes. Those were here when we got here."

Austin leaned in, his nose only a few inches above the ash tray, and inhaled. "They're fairly fresh. Last day or two."

"How can you tell?" Lucy asked.

"Like with fresh fish, the smell changes over time." Austin dangled the duct tape in front of the kids. "Know anything about this?"

"No," the boy said. "We don't."

"Here when you got here?" Austin asked.

They both nodded eagerly.

Lucy looked at Austin. "And they say they didn't even notice the car with the broken window."

The boy pointed. "We walked from that direction. I swear we would have called the police if we'd thought..."

"And you didn't see anyone?" Lucy asked.

They both shook their heads.

"Wait here," Lucy ordered, gesturing to the Toyota. "She pointed. I didn't see any shells, but there is a bullet hole in the back seat."

Austin opened the back door and examined the bullet hole, then looked back in the direction of the utility shed. "Car drives up and Wragg steps out of the shed. He shoots once to blow out the windshield, then a second time to kill the driver."

"I already called in the plates," Lucy said. "Benny Ramirez. Low-level guy at NCIS."

"Damn," Austin said.

"Why no shots fired on the second vehicle?" Jimmy asked.

Austin moved to inspect Sy's SUV. "The shooter killed

Ramirez immediately, then decided he needed a hostage. That's my hunch, anyway. Likely took off with Sy in his own car." He inspected the tire tracks on the dirt road. He thought he could make out the tracks of the Toyota and Sy's SUV, but he didn't see a third set of tracks leaving. "Or, maybe not."

Lucy headed back to the teenagers, who now sat cross-legged on the ground. A bright light cut through a gap in the trees, and they both shielded their eyes as Lucy stood over them. "Okay," she said, "we're gonna start this from the beginning."

Austin's phone vibrated in his pocket, a text from Samantha: *Thought you'd want to see this.*

Attached to the text was a link to a blog called *True Crime Addicts*. From the look of it, the site appeared to be a crummy blog that gave updates and opinions about whatever cases were hot in the news at the time.

He clicked through and found a short article titled: *Inside Edition Interview a Big Nothingburger.*

As he read the article, he wandered away from Lucy into the shade of an evergreen.

In case you missed the much-hyped Inside Edition interview with Maria Del Guado and Perry Diaz, you didn't miss much.

Del Guado is the widow of Adam Del Guado and, if reports are true, was paid handsomely for the interview, promising all sorts of revelations that would break the case wide open.

Instead, she offered up a bland retelling of things we already knew, as well as a smorgasbord of memories of her beloved Adam "Addie" Del Guado.

Our advice to Inside Edition, next time you pay big bucks to a widow, make sure she actually knows something.

He wandered back over to Lucy, who was still questioning the teenagers as Jimmy watched.

Part of him was relieved to hear that Maria Del Guado hadn't actually withheld anything to sell to TV. She'd been BS'ing *Inside*

Edition, using them for money. Then he stopped, scanning back up the document.

Addie.

Maria Del Guado called her husband "Addie."

He closed his eyes, replaying Vellory's recording of the night the three men had been killed.

Unless he was mistaken, the word he'd heard yelled into the night, barely audible over the howling wind, had been *Addie.*

CHAPTER THIRTY-ONE

WRAGG DROPPED to one knee and, eyes locked on Sy, used a long hunting knife to cut the duct tape from her feet. He left her wrists bound. Holding the knife up in front of her eyes, he licked his dry, cracked lips. "Try anything and I won't be nearly as nice to you at our next stop."

She kept her eyes blank, neutral.

Wragg stood and backed toward the door, eyes still on her. He set the hunting knife on a busted, three-legged table and pulled his pistol from its holster.

She'd never seen a gun like it. "That's the gun you used to shoot Adam Del Guado."

He looked down at his hand as though surprised to see the rare pistol there. He nodded.

She stood slowly, her legs stiff. Even the simple act of standing made her feel much better. "Why'd you kill him? What were you two arguing about? Or did someone hire you?" She paused. "Yeah, I'm guessing that's it."

He shook his head. "Stop talking." He glanced out the little window, looking down the slope that, she believed, led back to the utility shed where she'd been captured, back to her car.

"Did someone hire you? I have the authority to cut deals when the shooter is a pawn, like you are in this case."

He turned quickly. "I'm no pawn."

"You might think of yourself as a hired gun, even a badass killer. But you were hired by someone." She didn't know this to be true, but it was a possibility. One that she thought could rattle him.

He stepped toward her. "Shut your mouth, women."

"I heard you on the phone with your mom. That *was* your mom, right? I've found that even the hardest men turn into mushy babies around their mothers."

He leaned in, crouching slightly so his face was right in hers. He smelled of rotting teeth, cigarettes, and diesel fuel. Of filth. His thin brown hair clung to his neck, a mix of grease and sweat. "Another word—"

"And you'll kill me?"

He laughed, spittle hitting her face, and leaned in even closer. His nose brushed up against hers.

Everything inside her wanted to recoil, to pull back, but she held her face still.

"Killing you would be easy," he said, his voice wet and full of malice. "First I'm gonna do things you're going to like a lot less."

"Like what?" she whispered.

Without moving his face, he put his gun back in his holster. "Oh, you're about to find out."

She had no intention of finding out.

Jerking her head back suddenly, she swung it forward with the violence she'd been storing up for hours, maybe days, maybe years.

She connected, striking his nose with the top of her forehead.

In the little wooden hunting cabin, the sound of cracking cartilage was like beautiful music.

CHAPTER THIRTY-TWO

"EVER SEEN ANYONE ELSE UP HERE?" Lucy asked.

The teenagers both looked like they were going to be sick. Being caught half-naked by police was bad enough, but, judging by the scent, these two were high. Austin imagined that would make the whole interrogation much worse.

"Never," the girl said. "I mean, no one but, like, other teenagers."

"People come up here to drink beer and whatnot?" Lucy asked.

They both nodded.

Austin tuned them out, his mind darting in ten directions at once. Maria had said that only *she* called her husband Addie. So if Wragg had called him that while chasing him down the beach...

He thought back to her little house, to the ducks, to the way she spoke about money. The whole situation had been so ridiculous, perhaps he'd missed the most obvious conclusion of all. Most murders stemmed from either domestic disputes or money. It was quite possible that the murder of Adam Del Guado had come from a combination of the two.

He tuned back into Lucy's questioning when he heard one of the teenagers growing heated. "You never told me that!" It was the young man and he seemed more hurt than upset.

"It was none of your business," the girl said, defensively. "It was before we were going out."

Lucy was pushing them apart. "Wait, you..." she pointed at the young woman. "Where is this cabin?"

"Duh, it's like ten minutes that way." She pointed up the hill.

The young man looked crestfallen. "You went up there with Akiva? That guy is such a loser."

She sighed. "I said it was before I even knew you were into me."

The young man looked close to tears.

"Who owns the cabin?" Lucy demanded.

"It's like an abandoned shack almost," the girl said. "Kinda creepy. Deer antlers on the wall, like a hunting place or whatever. Has an old hunk of junk ATV out back. One time Akiva got it working and we drove up and around the mountain in it."

The young man was distraught. "Before you had *sex* with him!"

"Exactly which direction is it?" Austin demanded.

The young woman pointed straight up the mountain.

Lucy said, "I think that's still on the property of the gravel company."

Jimmy was already jogging up the hill, Austin close on his heels.

There was no doubt Jimmy was in better shape. He easily leapt over logs Austin had to slow down to climb over, and even after five minutes running uphill at something close to a sprint, he hadn't slowed. Dashing between trees and bounding over fallen branches, Jimmy was pulling away.

Austin, on the other hand, was panting, even with his adrenaline pumping.

Once or twice he tried calling to Jimmy to slow down, but it was no use.

He was already out of sight.

CHAPTER THIRTY-THREE

SY DIDN'T HAVE time to admire the blood spewing from Wragg's broken nose. She had more work to do.

When Wragg reached up instinctively to touch his face, this gave her the time she needed. She brought her knee up with all the force she had in her, leaping into the thrust and connecting with his groin.

Wragg toppled, crashing into the table, his head falling back and striking the floor as blood poured from his nose into his eyes.

The hunting knife slid off the table and landed at his side.

Wiping blood from his eyes, he reached for it, but she lunged and reached it first, gripping the cold metal just as she saw him reaching for his pistol.

Sy swiped the knife at his hand but hit only a glancing blow.

On his back, blood covering his face, he managed to get his gun free just as she dove on top of him.

The next moments were a chaotic scramble of blood and rage.

She pressed his arm down.

He headbutted her face.

She tried to stab his side.

He punched the side of her head.

He reached his gun. Brought it up.

She twisted his wrist.

Then she felt a hand on her other wrist. He was trying to grab the knife. Her face pressed up against the side of his gun, trying to push it away with her head and terrified it would go off at any second.

He kicked and swung his hips. She felt herself flying backwards. He'd launched her off using the leverage of his body against the ground.

As she hit the floor, she realized she still had the knife in her hand. She lunged as he raised the gun and fired.

Strangely, she wasn't knocked back by the bullet. It hit her like a needle, through her side. In and out.

A strange moment of lucidity struck her. Like everything had paused.

The next thing she knew she was crashing down on top of him, thrusting the hunting knife into his chest with a power and violence that seemed to come from a place within her she'd never known was there.

Tumbling to the floor, she glanced over and saw the knife sticking out of a spot between his shoulder and chest.

He was still. Her training told her to check if he was dead. To flee. To find his cellphone and call for help.

But instead a confusion closed in around her, the room spun, and everything went black.

CHAPTER THIRTY-FOUR

AUSTIN STUMBLED OVER A TREE ROOT, falling face-first into a nest of beer cans and cigarette butts. He leapt up, brushing himself off, and continued running.

"Austin, hurry!" It was Jimmy's voice, calling from further up the hill.

Austin reached him a minute later.

"Inside," Jimmy said. "Two bodies."

Austin looked through the window. His stomach twisted. "Sy."

"The door is locked," Jimmy said.

Austin hurried up to it, planted his left leg in the dirt, and kicked his right forward, connecting an inch to the left of the brass doorknob.

The door busted open and Jimmy ran through, crouching next to Sy. "She's alive."

Austin was at the wrist of Wragg, who had a knife between his right pectoral and shoulder. "So is he. Lotta blood. He won't be alive for long."

He knelt over Sy, examining the wound in her side. "Can you hear me? Symone?" He touched her shoulder. "Sy?"

"How do we get them out of here?" Jimmy said, his voice urgent.

Austin had an idea. "Ambulances can't get up here. Call them. Call Lucy. Get them to meet us back at the utility shed. Bolting out the front door, he ran around the side to the back of the cabin. Next to a wood pile was a large tarp covered in leaves. Yanking it off, he saw the ATV. No key, and it might take a while to hotwire it.

Back in the shack, Jimmy was using a roll of paper towels— the only clean thing he could find—to bandage Sy's wound. He'd moved all of the weapons into a pile beside him.

Austin scanned the room for keys. The hook by the door was empty, the table had been knocked over, and the floor covered in a layer of dirt and grime, but no keys.

He knelt by Wragg and patted down the pockets of his grimy jeans. Bingo. Something hard. He squeezed his hand into the pocket and yanked out a set of keys.

As he did, Wragg moved suddenly. A hand gripped Austin's wrist.

Austin swung his other hand around, breaking the grip. Wragg went limp. His eyes were closed. He appeared to be coming in and out of consciousness. "Keep an eye on him," Austin said, heading for the door.

A moment later, he had the ATV parked out front. Together, he and Jimmy carried Sy out the door and lay her on the ground.

Austin jumped into the driver's seat. "Lay her across my lap. It's the only way."

Carefully, Jimmy crouched and picked up Sy's semi-limp body, one arm supporting her neck, the other under her knees. With his strength, lifting her lean frame was easy.

As Jimmy lay her across Austin's lap, Sy made a weak sound, like a groan that got stuck in her throat.

Her legs dangled off one side and Austin held her head in his right hand, his left on the steering wheel. "I'll be back for Wragg. Keep that bastard alive if you can."

With that, he took his foot off the brake and let the ATV down the hill.

CHAPTER THIRTY-FIVE

FOUR HOURS LATER, Austin tossed a granola bar wrapper in the trash and washed it down with a sip of the worst coffee he'd ever tasted. Even for a hospital, this coffee was bad.

Sy's surgery had been going on for a couple hours, and there wasn't yet any news.

The ambulance had arrived only ten minutes after Austin had reached the utility shed and, thankfully, they'd been able to keep her alive on the ride to the hospital.

Only six doors down, a security guard sat outside the room of Davey Wragg. He'd received the best care the county could provide. His shoulder had been mended, his body pumped full of painkillers.

He was unconscious, but alive, and handcuffed to the bed.

Austin had listened to the brief conversation he'd had with Lucy and Jimmy before passing out. He'd given them nothing, admitted to nothing, and demanded a lawyer. The only other thing he'd said was that he planned to sue the Navy, NCIS, the state of Washington, and every public official therein. "Ain't no women can stab me and get away with it," he'd said. Apparently, he believed that Sy stabbing him entitled him to significant financial compensation.

Now Austin paced the hallway, thinking of all the things he'd done wrong that had brought him to this point.

"I can tell you're beating yourself up," Lucy said, coming up behind him. "Don't."

Austin turned.

"I was stuck on Vellory from the beginning," Austin said. "Him killing those young men to cover up his other crimes made too much sense." He struck the wall with an open palm.

Lucy put a hand on his shoulder, trying to reassure him. "Maria Del Guado. I was in her house, too. I didn't see it either. That is, assuming you're right."

Austin had explained to Lucy what he'd heard on the recording, Wragg's use of the nickname "Addie." Lucy had sent two officers to Maria Del Guado's house to bring her in for questioning, and asked Daniels to request a search warrant for her home, though Austin knew they were unlikely to get one given their lack of real evidence.

"What I don't get," Lucy said, "is this: Maria Del Guado hires Wragg to kill her husband, but why? Maybe because she's already seeing Perry?"

Austin paced the cold hallway. "Wouldn't be the first time a woman had her husband killed to claim his death benefit before moving on with her secret lover."

"Won't be the last, either. But here's what I don't get: Joey Blake and Hammer. Why involve them in this?"

Austin had run this over in his head a hundred times, and while he wasn't sure, he had a theory. "The recording. My sense is that Vellory arranged to meet with all three men. Maybe one of them wanted to come clean or whatever. Remember, they'd all been at the bar that night. So they are all going to meet there. Wragg follows Del Guado, maybe parks nearby the beach or somehow gets him to pull over. Del Guado runs away from

Wragg and *toward* the beach where he thinks he can get help. Wragg catches up with him, shoots him, then takes out the others because they happened to be witnesses."

"Can I quote you on that?" It was Anna Downey. She'd somehow crept up on them unnoticed.

He turned. "No!"

She stepped back. "I was *kidding*. Jeez!"

Lucy looked at her, arms folded. "You'll forgive us for not having the utmost faith in you after what happened."

Anna scanned the hallway. "I'll forgive you. Can *you* forgive *me?*"

Austin glanced at Lucy, who looked at the floor.

"I'm quick to forgive," Austin said. "But she has to run this department now, and I don't imagine you'll have a lot of luck getting scoops from her anytime soon."

Anna pointed at the guard stationed by Wragg's door. He'd taken a seat and seemed to be dozing off. "The perp is in there, I assume?"

"No comment," Lucy said.

Anna took out her notebook. "It's Wragg, right? The guy who, well, you know..."

Austin made his lips into a tight line.

Lucy said, "I can neither confirm nor deny that. And you can put that notebook away."

Anna frowned. "What's it gonna take for me to win back your trust?"

Lucy finally looked up. "Probably time."

A doctor in a white coat approached. "Are any of you Thomas Austin?"

"I am," Austin said.

"Symone Aoki is out of surgery. She's asking for you."

CHAPTER THIRTY-SIX

SY'S EYES flicked open as Austin walked in the room. She looked tired, but more peaceful, more at ease than he'd seen her before. Like Austin had been in the NYPD, Sy was someone who had a tough time relaxing away from work. With people like them, he thought, sometimes it took an illness or bullet wound to force some time away from the job.

"Hey," she said. Her voice was weak, but she seemed fully alert. Her black hair contrasted with the white pillow and hospital gown.

"Hey," Austin replied. "How are you?"

"Lucky. Bullet missed everything important. I'm groggy, but fine." She was covered by a thin blanket, but Austin could see the bulge by her right side, where her wound had been bandaged.

"Do you want to talk about what happened?" Austin asked. "I heard about your man. Benny?"

Her eyes closed tight. "I shouldn't have let him arrive before me. I *told* him to wait back, but..." Her hands wrung the blanket like she was squeezing out a sponge. "I never should have let him..."

"You can't blame yourself," Austin said. "Blame the guy down the hall."

Sy's eyes popped open. "He's *here?*"

"He lived. Bastard has the best doctors in the state to keep him alive. Handcuffed to a bed, but gets away with a million dollar view, same as yours." Austin pulled back the blinds, revealing the massive ice-clad peaks of the Olympic Mountains in the distance.

"Yeah, the least they could have done was give him a room facing the parking lot." She shook her head slowly. "I wish he'd died. I know I'm not supposed to say that. I know I'm supposed to want to bring him in alive, but..."

"You missed his heart by a few inches."

She thought for a moment, then said, "I want to explain what was going on. You deserve that."

Austin shook his head. "It can wait."

"No." With great effort, wincing with pain, she pushed herself up, managing to raise herself a little straighter against the headboard. "Now that it's all over, you should know."

Austin pulled up a chair and sat next to the bed. "Okay."

"The day I went to the scene with you and Ridley..." she stopped, as though just remembering something. "Ridley? Is it true he got put on leave?"

"Afraid so."

Sy closed her eyes. "That's my fault, too."

"No, it isn't. He knew *exactly* what he was doing. God could have come down from heaven and told him to drop the case, and Ridley would have done what Ridley does."

She smiled sadly. "But he wouldn't have had to do it if..." she let out a pained sigh. "Look, after I went to the scene with you I got a call."

Her voice was growing quieter and Austin leaned in. "From who?"

"From a person you don't *not* take a call from. I can't say who.

He told me two things. He told me about the Vellory scandal that was going to come out in the press. And he told me Vellory had nothing to do with the murders. Wanted me to act accordingly. Protect Vellory and find the real killer."

Austin considered this, figuring that the call must have come from one of a handful of people. The Secretary of the Navy, someone high up in the Pentagon, maybe even the President.

"This was a tricky situation," she continued. "Politically fraught. Above my pay grade. I was told to solve the murders without embarrassing the Navy too badly, and to leave Vellory out of it. Corruption thirty years ago is one thing. Murder is something else. I think Vellory knew he was cooked. He'd already come clean about the recording to his superiors, come clean about everything. A decision was made that he could go down for the corruption, but since he could prove he wasn't a murderer, well, the wagons were circled."

Austin wanted to object, but he was aware how fragile she looked. She didn't look like she had much energy to continue.

She squinted at him. "It turns out, I was *right*, too. Vellory wasn't the killer."

"Did Wragg say anything, give anything away?"

"No, but my hunch is it goes back to Del Guado's wife."

Austin smiled.

"What?"

"That's where we landed, too. We have officers on the way to her place right now. What gave it away for you?"

Sy adjusted her arm, grimacing in pain. "Hunch. Once I knew Wragg was the shooter, I thought back on the files. The fact that Del Guado's widow remarried so quickly after his death." Her head slipped down the side of the pillow, only a foot or two from Austin's face. "How long ago did your wife die?"

"Almost two years."

"And my husband died four years ago. Moving on hasn't been

easy." Her voice had grown soft. "No way I could move on the way Mrs. Del Guado did."

"Me neither," Austin said.

Sy's arm fell off the side of the bed and landed on his leg. She squeezed his knee—the weakest, lightest squeeze he'd ever felt.

"Do you think you'll ever be able to move on?" she asked. Her eyes were closed, her voice was sleepy.

Austin lowered his voice, too. "I'll never move on, but life will *go* on. I'll try to go with it. There's no other choice."

"What's the alternative, right?" She took his hand and tugged gently.

He leaned in.

She kissed him once, so softly it was almost as though it hadn't happened.

Pop pop pop.

Austin sat upright, letting go of her hand.

Gunshots.

He heard a commotion in the hallway. "Wait here."

He ran out, shutting the door to Sy's room behind him. Glancing up and down the hallway, he saw the security guard who'd been stationed outside Wragg's door. He was running down the hallway as though chasing someone, but the someone he was chasing was out of sight.

Austin raced down the hall and poked his head into Wragg's room. A doctor stood over him, mouth open. Stunned.

A nurse sobbed, hands over her mouth.

Wragg's body lay motionless, his wrists still handcuffed to the metal bars of the hospital bed.

Brain matter and blood covered the pillow and headboard. Half of his head had been blown off.

PART 3

BE BAD, BUT IN A
GOOD WAY

CHAPTER THIRTY-SEVEN

IT TOOK Austin twenty minutes to piece together what had happened.

While he was speaking with Sy, a man had entered the hospital and casually walked up one flight of stairs to the second floor. The security guard had been inattentive outside David Wragg's room. The man had rushed past, shot Wragg in the head, then fled. The guard had pursued him, joined by two officers who happened to be patrolling outside the hospital.

The shooter had a car waiting out front, driven by someone else, and they'd escaped, pursued by the officers. As far as Austin knew, the pursuit was still ongoing.

Lucy and Jimmy were working with hospital security to look over surveillance footage, but, according to witnesses, the shooter had been a male of average height and he'd been wearing a baseball hat and a mask, so they couldn't describe much about his features.

Description or no, Austin thought he knew who it was. Still, there was nothing he could do. Nothing but wait.

After telling Sy what had happened and coaxing her back to sleep, he headed down to the hospital cafeteria, where he found

Anna typing on her laptop and sipping a green smoothie from a plastic bottle.

She must have seen him approaching because, without looking up, she asked, "We friends again?"

"Tentatively," Austin said, biting into an apple. "How come you're still here?"

"I don't know. I like to be where the action is. Something told me the day wasn't done. Turns out I was right. Any word on the shooter?"

Austin shook his head. "Did you see it go down?"

"No, I was down here. But I overheard a couple nurses talking about it. What do you think?"

Austin frowned. "You really think I'm gonna comment on the story I assume you're writing?"

She closed her laptop. "Fair enough. A peace offering: I was researching Maria Del Guado and her husband, Perry. Perry has a small chain of gyms, three or four total, right?"

Austin nodded.

"His gym has endorsements from a former Navy Seal and caters to the community of people looking for extreme training." She eyed him over the bottle as she finished off her smoothie. "On the 'About' page of their website, it says that the gym's management consults with a former Navy Seal on every piece of equipment and on their signature exercise class, *Hell Week Daily*. I guess it's some extreme exercise thing."

"And you're thinking Davey Wragg is their consultant?"

Anna nodded.

Austin considered this, trying to look less interested than he was. Other than the word "Addie" shouted into the wind on a recording he'd probably never hear again, that was the best evidence he had of a connection between Maria and Perry and Davey Wragg.

Anna smiled. "I can tell from the look on your face that you agree, but don't want to say so. You've got a crummy poker face, New York."

"I have other evidence that connects Wragg to Maria and Perry. But..." he hesitated.

"Off the record." She shoved her closed laptop to the center of the table. "I swear. I want to figure this out as badly as you do."

"If Maria and Perry hired Wragg to kill Adam Del Guado, doesn't it seem like a giant damn coincidence that it went down the same night Vellory set up a meeting of the men on the beach?"

"Maybe," Anna said. "But coincidences happen all the time. Also possible Maria and Perry hired Wragg and he chose that particular night because he knew Perry would be out on the Bluff. No one to hear the gunshots."

"Definitely possible," Austin said, "but I still feel like we're missing something."

"Maybe, but... what are you thinking? Your eyes get this weird look when you have an idea."

She'd read him correctly. He did have an idea. "You owe me, right?"

Anna hesitated. "I mean, I *did* apologize profusely."

Austin leveled his gaze on her. "But you still owe me, and, more importantly, Lucy."

"Don't bring her into this."

Austin slid the laptop toward her. "How fast can you write a story?"

"Very, but what do you have in mind?"

She watched him, her frown increasing in direct proportion to his widening smile.

"Austin, what?"

He said, "Have you ever heard of 'Shaking the Suspect Tree'?"

"No."

"You're gonna hate it. It's when we plant a story in the newspapers, or online, just to see how a suspect reacts to it. Deception."

Anna was shaking her head. "Hell no. No way."

"Anna."

"No! That's disinformation. You might have been able to use the New York tabloids that way, but I don't—"

"Anna, please, hear me out. You wouldn't have to actually *publish* it. Write up a quick story—I'll tell you the main points—then send it to Vellory for comment. All you have to do is convince him that it's real, that it's going to come out and you're asking for his comment. Then we see what he does."

Anna was still skeptical. "You know that could get me fired, right?"

Austin nodded.

"Shouldn't we talk to Lucy?" she asked.

"Absolutely not. She'd never let this happen."

She scrunched up her nose at him. "Is this one of those, *When lives are on the line, I make the rules* moments?"

"You're never gonna let that go, are you?"

She smirked. "Probably not."

"Well, lives aren't on the line in this case. But three Navy men were murdered in cold blood and left to rot in a swampy marsh. I don't know about you, but I won't sleep well until I know the whole story."

She opened her laptop and let out a long, slow breath. "You and I are a lot alike."

Austin's phone rang. It was Lucy. "Hello?"

Her voice was full of excitement. "We sort of caught the shooter. Perry. Must have heard about Wragg's arrest and wanted to silence him."

"That's great," Austin said. "What did the 'sort of' mean?"

"He stopped on the Tacoma Narrows Bridge. He's on the other side of the railing, and he's threatening to jump. Jimmy and I are heading out. Where are you?"

"Cafeteria with Anna. Okay if I bring her?"

"Okay, but she'll owe us big time."

Austin stood. "Oh, she'll probably do us a favor down the line." He ended the call. "Let's go."

"What was that about?" Anna asked.

"Grab your laptop. Looks like you're about to get another scoop."

CHAPTER THIRTY-EIGHT

A WARM SUMMER rain had begun while they were in the hospital.

Anna tossed Austin the keys to her SUV. "You drive. I'll write. I think I know what you have in mind, but—"

"Don't worry," Austin said, hopping into the driver's seat, "I've got talking points."

They peeled out of the hospital parking lot, wipers on high, tires kicking up spray from the puddles. "The bridge is about twenty minutes away," Austin said. "Will that be enough time to write it?"

Anna pulled out her laptop. "I write fast. Gimme the gist."

Austin gave her five or six main points as Anna took notes, then she told him to be quiet so she could focus.

Austin weaved through traffic as fast as he could without being reckless. He wished Lucy was behind the wheel. He'd grown used to driving in New York, where traffic was much worse and one rarely got out on the open road. Here, there was more room, which made driving both easier and harder. Easier because you could get where you were going more quickly, but harder because swerving in and out of traffic at sixty miles an hour gave one a lot more opportunity to screw up.

When they were a couple minutes from the bridge, Anna looked up, studied her screen for a moment, then said, "The point of this is to see how he'll react, right?"

"Right. What do you have?"

"Just to be clear: I would never publish this, and it goes against everything I stand for."

Austin nodded.

"I'm only doing this because I think he's guilty as hell."

"And you owe me one," Austin pointed out.

"And that."

Anna cleared her throat and read.

David Wragg, Possible Shooter in Memorial Day Massacre, Killed in Hospital. Suspect at Large. High-Ranking Admiral Being Investigated as Accomplice in Triple Homicide

In a shocking series of developments in the investigation surrounding the triple homicide that took place on Memorial Day, 1992, the suspected shooter, Hansville resident Davey Wragg, was killed today only hours after his arrest.

Police have not yet verified the identity of the shooter, though sources close to the case believe it to be Perry Diaz — the current husband of Maria Del Guado, widow to one of the deceased, Adam Del Guado.

In other developments, multiple sources within the Kitsap Sheriff's Department say that Wragg did not act alone. "Evidence in the public domain has already linked the three deceased men to the well-publicized case involving fraud and kickbacks during Operation Desert Storm," one source said. "That scandal, masterminded by Admiral Tom Vellory, may well be tied to their deaths."

Another source went even further. "Admiral Vellory is a suspect in our murder investigation at this time. We believe he may have played a part in the killings in order to cover up his other crimes."

She stopped reading and looked over. "So?"

Austin thought through the article. The truth was, it was perfect. But something inside him knew that sending it violated a dozen rules and ethical guidelines, both in Anna's line of work, and in his.

The irony wasn't lost on him. In the days after the medals and bones were found in the marshlands, the Navy, and perhaps Vellory's own people, had flooded the internet with disinformation to try to confuse the issue. Now, he and Anna were going to spread a little disinformation of their own.

He said, "If that doesn't get his attention, I don't know what will."

"Send it?"

Austin gripped the steering wheel tight. They were about a mile from the bridge when he saw an ocean of red tail lights ahead of him. "Send it." All traffic heading toward the bridge appeared to have stopped. They weren't getting any closer.

He waited until he heard the *whoosh* of her outgoing email, then said. "Thanks, Anna. I know you didn't want to do that. I didn't either." He pulled over to the side of the highway. "You up for a jog in the rain?"

They got out and, hugging the wall along the side of the highway, began jogging toward the bridge. After a couple minutes, the rain soaked through Austin's clothes, mingling with sweat.

On a clear summer day, the Tacoma Narrows Bridge was one of the prettiest Austin had ever seen. A set of twin suspension bridges, it spanned the Tacoma Narrows strait over the Puget Sound, connecting the city of Tacoma with the Kitsap Peninsula.

As they approached, he saw the lights at the top of the bridge first, then the rest slowly came into view. It looked nothing like the picturesque bridge he'd fallen in love with.

At night, in the heavy downpour, with flashing lights everywhere and traffic stopped, it looked like a war zone or the scene of a crime.

CHAPTER THIRTY-NINE

THE SCENE WAS CHAOTIC, but in the center of the bridge, things were strangely calm. Cars had stopped in both lanes, but a small perimeter had been set up near the center of the bridge—three ambulances and a ring of paramedics and officers.

Austin spotted Lucy's red hair, damp and illuminated by the bridge lights. She stood about a yard from the railing on the edge of the bridge.

He followed her gaze to Perry, who had climbed over the railing. With one arm he clung to the railing. In his free hand he held a gun. Austin had been confronted with two suicide attempts in his life. In the first one, he'd managed to keep the woman talking long enough that she'd had second thoughts and come down from the roof. The other, he'd lost.

This one wasn't his responsibility, but he felt it just as acutely.

Sidling up beside Lucy, he asked, "What's the status?"

She pointed to a paramedic in a yellow jacket. "She's good. Specializes in this."

Over the sound of the rain pounding the metal bridge and splashing all around them, Austin couldn't hear what she was saying, but she appeared to be engaged in conversation with Perry. She had both hands up and was only a few feet from him. Around her, four others were poised. Listening. Waiting.

Lucy said, "Twenty minutes ago, he requested to see Maria. Said he'd jump if she didn't show up. He gave us her cellphone number and we have an officer escorting her here right now."

Austin was surprised. "She wasn't the driver when he fled the hospital?"

"Driver is already in custody. Jimmy is with him. Sounds like he didn't know what was going on. Teenager who works at one of Perry's gyms. He claims Perry told him he was going to visit his sick mother in the hospital."

Something about that fact sickened him. For the rest of his life, that kid would have to live with the fact that he'd been an unwitting accomplice to murder. Austin let his head fall back, allowing the rain to pound his face. He could make out individual droplets as they fell toward him, moving ever so slightly with the wind and lit by the bright lights of the bridge.

"Did Perry admit to killing Wragg?" he asked.

Lucy shook her head. "Not that I've heard. We already knew he did, but we got confirmation from the hospital. It's him on surveillance. We have his car pulling up, leaving. It's open and closed. Damn security guard was as useful as..." she sighed. "I'm too tired to think of an analogy."

She turned and Austin followed her eyes. An officer was leading Maria Del Guado down the bridge. She wore black jeans and a blue and green Seahawks jersey under a yellow raincoat. Her face was puffy and ashen, like she'd been up for days.

As the officer led her to the railing—where Perry still clung, his face desperate—Maria's knees buckled beneath her. She nearly collapsed, or at least, pretended to. She'd fooled everyone for thirty years, and Austin could no longer believe a single thing she said or did.

Taking the officer's arm for support, she made her way to the railing.

Austin and Lucy slowly crept forward, trying to get within earshot.

"Purr, don't do this," Maria said, her voice more angry than Austin had expected. "Get over here."

She reached out her hand, but Perry leaned away. "Tell them."

Maria glanced at the paramedics, then at Austin and Lucy. He couldn't be sure, but she didn't seem to remember them. Or, if she did, her eyes betrayed nothing.

"Come back to this side of the railing, baby. We can make this better."

Perry's voice trembled. His brown hair was soaked and water ran down his face, mingling with tears. "Tell them what you made me do."

Maria leaned away.

"Tell them or I'll jump!" His voice was a ragged howl that cut through the wind and rain.

Lucy inched forward. "Tell us, Maria."

Maria turned, looking at Lucy, then back at Perry. She stepped toward the railing and peered over the edge, as though contemplating something. It was a two hundred foot drop into dark, tumultuous waters.

Austin wondered whether she might be considering what the fall would do to her husband, or was she considering jumping herself? Finally, she stepped back, closed her eyes, and began to speak. "You really screwed us, Purr." As she continued, she adjusted strands of wet hair as though she could somehow undo the effects of the downpour. "Perry and I began seeing each other while Addie was still alive. Addie was *abusive*. He told me about what he and his pals did over in Iraq, then he beat me and made me promise not to tell anyone." She spat suddenly, violently, and her next words came out more as a hiss. "He *deserved* what he got." Gathering herself, she continued, "Perry and I made the plan. Perry knew Davey Wragg. They planned it all out. I'd let them know when Addie was going drinking in Hansville, and they'd take care of the rest. We wanted the Navy death benefit so we could start the first gym." She met eyes with Lucy. "I swear it had nothing to do with Joey or Hammer. Those other two..." She doubled over suddenly, sobbing.

Austin had seen this before. The weight of carrying a huge lie sometimes made people physically ill. And sometimes the relief of telling the truth was both emotional and physical.

"What about Vellory?" Lucy asked.

It took her a moment to gather herself. Again, she tried to neaten her hair, but the rain was coming down so hard her adjustments had no effect. "I barely knew who Vellory was. I mean, I knew he was their commander. I knew he was the ringleader of the stuff they did over in Iraq."

Lucy asked. "Could he have had anything to do with Hammer and Blake?"

"I swear I don't know what happened to those men. I always thought maybe Davey killed them, too, but I don't know. It was only supposed to be Addie."

Maria looked over at her husband.

Austin believed that Maria was telling the truth. She didn't know anything else about Vellory. But from the look on Perry's face, Austin could tell that he did.

CHAPTER FORTY

PERRY DROPPED his gun and watched as it fell into the darkness. It was much too loud to hear the splash as it disappeared in the water below.

He wrapped his second arm around the railing, then nodded at something the yellow-jacketed paramedic said. Two others approached and Perry allowed them to wrap a line under his arms and around his back, securing him to the railing.

It appeared as though he was willing to be saved, but not yet willing to come back to the other side of the railing.

Austin and Lucy crowded forward.

Despite the rain and the howling wind, Austin heard Perry's confession as though the man was whispering in his ear.

"Davey and I had it all worked out. We'd give him eight thousand dollars from the Navy death benefit when we got it. Maria would give me the go ahead, Davey would wait for him to leave the Watering Hole and do the job. Like I said, it was *all* worked out. A few days later, Davey came to me with a proposition." Perry's lips quivered. "I swear I didn't hire him to kill those other two." He paused a long time, then slowly composed himself and continued. "Davey said he'd made a side deal. He'd do the thing for only two grand, but we had to give him information. He wanted to know not only when Adam was going to the Watering Hole, but when he was meeting Hammer and Joey. I asked why. He said, don't worry about it. Someone else wants the other two gone. I needed that extra six grand. At least I thought I did. I asked Maria to tell me when Adam was going to meet the others. She told me. I told Davey. And that's all I know about what happened."

Somehow, Davey had known Tom Vellory thirty years ago. And through a random confluence of murderous evil, Vellory had been plotting to take out all three of his men around the same time that Maria and Perry were planning to kill Adam Del Guado.

Maria now sat on the road, head in her hands, probably getting used to the fact that she was about to spend twenty to life in prison.

As Perry allowed himself to be pulled back across the railing, Anna touched Austin's arm. "Take a look at this."

Austin had been so riveted by Perry's confession that he'd almost forgotten where he was. He turned.

Anna was holding up her cell phone, shielding it from the rain with her free hand. Vellory had replied to her fake article. They crowded in next to one of the ambulances, shielding themselves from the worst of the rain, which was now blowing in at an angle.

Dear Ms. Downey,

Talk to your editor. I just got you fired. He assured me that you never would have done something that stupid on your own. So who put you up to this? Someone at NCIS, someone in the Sheriff's Department?

"Do you think he's lying?" Anna asked.

Austin doubted it. "I'm sorry, I—"

She thought for a moment. "Screw it. It was a crappy job anyway, and the real scoop I published about Vellory was my most-read article ever, despite the fact that the big papers got the same story the next day. I have plenty of offers now. Should I write back?"

Austin said, "Tell him it was me."

"His message was sent only two minutes ago. I have a number for his house that I left a dozen messages at when I was reporting the original story about his corruption."

"Worth a shot," Austin said.

As Anna dialed, the wind picked up, whistling and howling. Austin thought he could feel the bridge swaying beneath him. He remembered pictures he'd seen from 1940, when the bridge had swayed wildly in a windstorm and collapsed. Thankfully, they'd built it back much stronger. The only casualty in the collapse had been a dog named Tubby. He thought of Run and wished he were home with her.

Anna snapped to get his attention. Vellory had answered.

She crouched low, pressing the phone into her ear so Austin could only hear her side of the conversation. "Thomas Austin," she said. "Yes, that's right. The story would have broken anyway... yes I know I was the first to publish, but the *Times* and the *Post* had it as well. You can bet they were going to run it, I just beat them to it.... Yes, yes. *Thomas Austin*.... Okay, I'll ask. Hold on."

She muted the phone, checked the surrounding area, then leaned in. "He says he wants to meet with you. Tonight. Alone."

Austin cocked his head, thinking. "Why?"

"He's had his book and TV contracts canceled. New stories of his corruption are popping up every day. Perry's confession implicates him, though he doesn't know that yet. His was already set to be one of the worst downfalls of a major American military figure of all time. My guess is that he knows he's going down for the murders as well."

"Okay, I'm right there with you, but why would he want to speak with me?"

Anna considered this. "Honestly, I have no idea. But how can you refuse?"

Austin nodded and Anna got back on the phone. "He'll be there in an hour."

When she ended the call, Austin said, "Are you going to come?"

"He said 'alone.'"

Austin leaned against the ambulance. "What I ought to do right now is go tell Lucy. About the fake article. About the call. The meetup. Let her decide what to do."

"Then why aren't you doing that?"

Austin looked out past the cars, past the bridge, past where the lights stopped hitting the raindrops and into a darkness that hung over the water like death. The truth was, he didn't know the answer.

There wasn't a good answer.

But something in him knew he had to see this through.

Austin said goodbye to Lucy, who was working with the paramedics and officers to get Perry and Maria basic medical attention before, presumably, taking them to the station for questioning, booking, and jail.

Anna told him she'd get a ride home from another reporter who'd just come to the scene. She gave him her keys and offered an overly-formal handshake. "If anything interesting happens, I get the scoop, okay?"

"Deal," Austin said. "I did just cost you your job, after all."

He said goodbye and began the mile walk back to Anna's SUV, but on the way past Lucy's cruiser, he stopped. Finding it unlocked, he popped the trunk and borrowed a bullet proof vest.

He'd been carrying his gun all day and doubted very much that he'd need it. Still, he had no idea what Vellory was up to, and he certainly wasn't going to go in unprepared.

CHAPTER FORTY-ONE

VELLORY'S HOUSE was dark except for an orange glow coming from the second story office. Austin got out of the car, his footsteps crunching loudly on the gravel parking lot.

On his ride from the bridge, the rain had stopped, but the air was thick, the night dark, as though the storm was simply taking a break before unleashing its fury again.

"Thomas *Austin*. Fitting that it would be you."

The voice from the porch startled him. Austin stopped at the top step as Vellory, who'd been sitting on an old wooden rocking chair, stood.

"Why do you say that?" Austin asked.

"Come inside and I'll explain. Everything."

At the top of the stairs, Austin paused, waiting for Vellory to open the door. For a long time, he just stood, motionless. Suddenly Vellory turned, grabbing Austin's wrist and twisting it behind his back. In the same motion, Vellory unholstered Austin's gun, which he had positioned on his right hip. Letting go of his wrist, Vellory tossed the gun into the bushes well off the porch. "I was the best close combat man in the Navy for a long time," he said.

Austin gathered himself, taking a step back. "I see that your skills haven't grown rusty."

"Don't worry," Vellory said. "If I wanted you dead I would have shot you from the porch. But I couldn't have you bringing a weapon into my home. My wife is sleeping."

Vellory had been quick, especially for his age. And he'd caught Austin off guard. Despite the fact that Vellory was clearly capable of murder, Austin hadn't felt especially worried. After all, Vellory had asked him to his home. And he likely already knew that both local police and the Navy itself were coming for him. Killing Austin would do nothing to stop the avalanche of disaster rolling down hill towards him.

Vellory flicked on a porch light and Austin saw that he was wearing his dress blues. Navy blue suit coat—double-breasted, with six gold buttons—and matching wool trousers. The shirt was bright white, contrasting with the black tie secured with a four-in-hand knot. His hair was perfectly styled, as though it had been cut that very day.

Everything about his appearance was immaculate, except for his expression. He had his usual confident, almost cocky smile, but there was a weariness underneath that he couldn't hide. A weariness, Austin thought, that can only come from decades spent pretending to be something other than what you really are.

Austin followed him up the stairs. He noticed that Vellory walked quietly, as though trying not to wake his wife. Despite everything, he was trying to be considerate.

When he closed the door behind them in the office, he offered Austin a leather chair at a large oak desk. Austin sat.

Vellory took the chair on the other side. "You're probably wondering why I invited you here."

Austin surveyed the room, which was empty save for the two of them. "I can't say I wasn't surprised. Did you really get Anna Downey fired?"

Vellory nodded. "There's something I taught my men that I

never spoke about publicly. If you find yourself outmanned, outgunned, and you are certain you are going down, take out as many enemies as you can along the way. Kamikaze, the Japanese called it. You could call it brave, or heroic, but it's just a more efficient way to run a unit. It puts other men's lives at less risk." He paused. "Anna Downey helped bring me down. She won. But I wouldn't be doing my duty if I didn't take her out on my way down. Might save another great man from a similar fate."

Austin decided to ignore the fact that he'd just referred to himself as a *great man*. "She's not your enemy, and neither am I. All we wanted was to find out what happened to Adam Del Guado, Jack Hammeron, and Joey Blake. Those three men deserve justice."

Pain joined the exhaustion on Vellory's face. "They do."

Something in the way he said it made Austin think he truly believed it. "What am I doing here?"

Vellory reached for something in an open drawer to his right. Austin flinched, almost bolted for the door.

It was a stack of file folders.

Vellory slid them across the desk. "Further evidence of my crimes. Everything that's already out there is a fraction of what I did. It's all here."

Austin flipped through a few pages. Receipts, invoices, letters, all dated between 1988 and 1997. It was too much to take in. They looked real, but it would take days or weeks to go through it all. Possibly longer to figure out what it all meant.

"Why?" Austin asked. "Why give me these?"

"Kitsap Sheriff's department has a warrant for my arrest. They'll be coming by in the morning. Doesn't sound like they have any solid evidence yet, but I don't intend to be around while they look for it."

Austin stiffened, sat up straight, and locked in on Vellory's pale blue eyes. "What do you want me to do with these papers?"

"Take photos of all of them. Send them to your friend, Anna."

Austin was shocked. "You can't be serious."

"Those documents prove that all the stories about me are true. More importantly: they prove that the Navy had *nothing* to do with it." He folded his arms. "Please, right now. Before I change my mind."

Austin thought of Anna. Having just lost her job, there was likely nothing she'd enjoy more than a trove of documents that would secure her spot as the leading source of news on one of the biggest stories in the world.

"I'm going to reach for my phone," Austin said. "This could take a while."

CHAPTER FORTY-TWO

TWO HOURS LATER, Austin's wrist was beginning to hurt from the repetition of taking photos, attaching them to emails, and sending them to Anna.

She'd tried calling him after the first few messages arrived, but Vellory insisted that he not answer. When Austin had sent the final email, he slid the documents back to Vellory.

The Admiral had watched him the whole time, his face shifting from placid, to pained, and back to placid a dozen times. "You know what else is in those documents?" Vellory asked. "They prove that I forced my men to go along with my crimes, including Del Guado, Hammeron, and Blake. I *made* them go along with it."

"Did they threaten to confess, and that's why you had them killed?"

Vellory let out a long sigh. "I believed at the time that my importance to the Navy, to the United States, was worth the lives of those three men. I wasn't wrong, even if what I did was wrong. So I paid that greasy piece of crap Wragg." He paused, lifting a paperweight from the desk, a piece of glass shaped to look like a grenade. "Be bad, but in a good way. That's what average people will never get about what men like me do. We commit great crimes in the service of a greater good. That's what war is."

"You weren't at war with Hammer, Del Guado, or Blake. They were *your* men."

He slammed down the paper weight, splitting it in two. "They were going to rat me out just to be *honest*. If I'd been taken down in 1992, America would have been weaker. More men would have died as a result. The second Iraq War, Afghanistan. I saved more lives than I took."

"That's a twisted logic I'll never understand."

"No, Thomas Austin. You won't."

"I grew up around the Navy. I know people who love it, and the country, as much as you claim to. They never would have done what you did."

"They never had my power," Vellory barked. "My responsibility. And I know you grew up around the Navy."

This caught Austin off guard. "Is that what you meant when you said it was fitting that it was me? A Navy brat who never served, bringing down one of America's most beloved Admirals?"

"I thought I recognized the name Austin when you were here with that detective. I knew your mom." His tone was whispery, lecherous.

Austin froze. He'd taken what he'd learned about his mom and Captain Garrison and stuffed it into the *do-not-open* drawer in his mind. Suddenly, it all came back, along with dozens of memories he'd barely known were there. Cold, wordless dinners between his parents. Separate bedrooms. Snide comments from his father that he'd been too young to understand.

He blinked, trying to regain his focus. "So what?"

"I did two years in San Diego. Ninety-six and ninety-seven, I believe." He waited until Austin met his eyes. "Guys on that base passed your mom around like a Tunisian whore."

Before he knew what he was doing, Austin leapt up and lunged across the desk.

Vellory was just as quick. As Austin grabbed Vellory's collar, he felt something hard pressing into his belly. He glanced down as he cocked his fist.

"Don't," Vellory said. He held a pistol up to Austin's stomach.

Austin raised his hands and slowly sat back into the chair.

Vellory relaxed, holding the gun just above the desk, finger on the trigger. It was a nickel-plated .45, similar to Austin's own firearm of choice. "Didn't your father clean our ships or something?"

"He was a contractor," Austin said, more defensively than he'd hoped. "He cleaned and repaired vessels for the Navy for forty years."

Vellory laughed. "He was so clueless. Everyone mocked him."

Austin said nothing.

"Your mom, though... my only regret, thinking back on it, is that I never had a go at her." He shook his head, pale blue eyes locked in on Austin as though gauging his reaction.

Austin stared right back. "You talk about honor and country. All you do is honor yourself. Your books, your TV appearances. All of it."

Vellory said nothing.

Austin continued, "And if you're through honoring yourself for a minute, how about we get to why I'm really here."

"You're here as a conduit. To get the truth out. It's important to me to leave with honor, to leave the Navy unscathed."

Austin wanted to explain why that was impossible. The crimes Vellory had committed and had forced his men to commit had embarrassed the Navy and would weaken its standing internationally. When news broke that a two-star Admiral had participated in the murder of his own men to cover it up.... Well, in a world where news stories came and went day to day, this one would have staying power. Even if his documents showed that others in the Navy were innocent, the Navy itself would take a major hit.

"Wait," Austin said. "What do you mean 'leave'?"

"I'm going to kill myself." Vellory said it as though there was nothing to it.

Austin froze, studying his face. He appeared to be absolutely serious. "You can still regain your honor—some of it—by admitting what you did in court. They deserve to hear it from you. Think of Hammer Junior."

Vellory seemed to be considering this. His eyes were searching and yet somehow far away. "No," he said at last. "The documents you sent will clear the Navy, clear my men. I won't go to prison. This is the only way." He glanced down at the gun, which was still pointed at Austin, then looked up. "Remember what I said about taking out as many enemies as you can on the way out?"

Without breaking eye contact, Vellory fired.

Austin rocked back, struck in the chest. Crashing to the floor, he rolled onto his stomach as the pain tore through his chest and ribs.

Face against the cold wooden floor, he looked up at Vellory out of a single half-open eye.

Then Vellory lifted the .45 slowly, held it in front of his face, and jammed it in his mouth. Austin's eyes began watering. He could barely see, but he didn't want to move. He listened for the shot.

Silent, still, he listened.

And listened.

It didn't come.

Vellory was a blur of Navy blue. Austin blinked, trying to clear his eyes. Finally, Vellory came into focus, his face quivering and full of indecision.

He couldn't do it, Austin thought. Vellory had decided to do what he thought was the honorable thing: clear the Navy of any wrongdoing and take his own life while killing Austin on his way out.

But he hadn't been able to go through with it.

Vellory stood suddenly and disappeared from Austin's view.

All he heard were heavy footsteps bounding across the wooden floor, then hurrying down the stairs.

CHAPTER FORTY-THREE

AUSTIN REACHED FOR HIS CHEST. The bulletproof vest had caught the round, but the force of it had been enough to leave him shocked. No doubt there would be a bruise the size of a grapefruit on his chest by tomorrow.

He stood, wobbling and stumbling toward the desk.

Bracing himself, he scanned the room for another weapon, but saw nothing. Vellory had taken the pistol.

As he stood, the pain in his chest worsened. It throbbed, like any blow would, but the pain had an acuity, a piercing sharpness that told him the force might have chipped his sternum. He tried to pull the bullet out of the vest, but it was lodged too deep.

Leaning into the light, he saw that it was a serrated, hollow-point bullet. Designed specifically to kill.

Gathering himself, he bolted out of the room and down the stairs.

At the bottom of the stairs he saw that floodlights now lit the front and side of the house.

On the porch, he stopped. Thinking. Listening.

The lights of a car appeared on the road leaving Vellory's house.

No, not leaving. He hadn't heard a car start.

Those were headlights coming *toward* the house. It was a white SUV, but not Anna's. That was Sy. He didn't have time to wait for a friendly greeting.

Austin leapt down the steps, turning left, running past his car, then careening around the side of the porch. Bright flood-lights cast sharp beams across the wide lawn near the house, leaving the rest of the lawn in darkness. But Austin had seen it through the window on their first visit. He knew the grass stretched all the way down to the water, to the dock.

Then another patch of grass grew bright and Austin saw him. Vellory was running for the water, setting off motion-detector lights as he ran. Every ten yards or so, a new light clicked on, likely set up to catch motion all the way from the water's edge to the house.

Vellory may have been a better hand-to-hand fighter than Austin, but his run was lumbering and stiff. Even with a cracked sternum, Austin knew he could catch him.

He took off at a jog, careful not to slip on the soaked grass. Lush as it was, it was free of mud, but it was spongy and slippery. He was maybe fifty yards behind Vellory when the Admiral reached the water and began untying his boat.

Austin slipped, slid forward, moisture splattering his face. Looking up from the ground, he saw Vellory throwing a rope onto the boat and climbing aboard.

Austin pressed himself up and ran, reaching the water's edge as the boat eased away from the shore.

He leapt, feeling the air whoosh past him as though flying. He crashed into the side of the boat, his chest striking the side. His torso throbbed in pain as the bullet, still lodged in the vest, pressed into the wreckage that was his sternum.

He barely got both arms over the edge of the vessel. His whole lower half dangled in the water. Kicking furiously, he pulled himself up over the side of the boat.

But before he could even hit the deck, Vellory was over him, swinging the butt of the pistol into Austin's jaw.

CHAPTER FORTY-FOUR

AUSTIN HAD LEARNED EARLY on that, in a fight, sometimes the only way to get the upper hand was to absorb a non-fatal blow in the short term in order to gain a stronger position overall. As he watched the butt of the pistol coming toward his face —in an instantaneous calculation—he realized that, if he could absorb it and remain conscious, he'd have the upper hand.

His head jolted sideways as the gun smashed into his jaw. He couldn't see, but he reached out his arm and gripped Vellory's ankle, using his momentum and pulling hard as he simultaneously kicked out his legs to trip Vellory's other leg.

Vellory tumbled, dropping the gun, which tumbled across Austin's shoulder and onto the deck.

Austin rolled on top of him, absorbing a glancing elbow to the ribs and taking hold of Vellory's head.

Vellory kicked his legs, almost rocking Austin off him. But Austin steadied himself and gripped Vellory's hair, which was still stiff with gel. Once, twice, Austin bashed Vellory's head into the deck, but Vellory was able to turn his head slightly to avoid the full force of the blow.

After the third time his head hit the deck, Vellory used

Austin's weight against him, rolling over on top of him, pressing his elbow right into the bullet still lodged in the vest. Austin gasped for air as Vellory pressed his forearm down into his throat.

Then Vellory made a mistake. Pressing his forearm down to try to choke Austin out, he shifted his weight slightly.

Austin thrust his hips up and twisted, knocking Vellory off him.

As Vellory struggled to turn, Austin grabbed the pistol and smashed the back of the Admiral's head with the butt of the weapon.

Vellory crumbled. On his knees, Austin raised the gun to strike him again, but Vellory had gone completely limp. Austin watched his motionless body for what felt like minutes, maybe hours, but was probably only a few seconds.

Austin wobbled, then collapsed. He lay still, listening to the sound of his own ragged breath, too numb to feel the pain he knew must be pulsing through his body.

Everything around him grew bright. He squinted, walking on his knees to the edge of the boat and looking over the side. Twenty yards away, another boat drifted toward him. Through tears and sweat and blood, he couldn't see much. But as he blinked he thought he caught a glimpse of Sy standing behind the wheel of a small motorboat.

He thought about the kiss. Had that been real? It seemed ages ago, if it had happened at all.

He fell back to the deck, staring up at the sky. It was as black as a sky could get, he thought. As he had a few days earlier, he tasted mushrooms and miso, seaweed and steak. All the earthy, umami flavors. They'd always been flavors he'd found difficult to describe, just like the emotion he was experiencing.

The boat drifted gently.

"Austin?" It was Sy's voice, at least he thought so. It had to

be, but she sounded different, further away. Or maybe *he* was
further away.

When he'd been walking down the trail to Foulweather Bluff
with Ridley and Sy, it had felt like the weight of history had been
brought into the present moment. Birth, death, all his past and
present, along with that of everyone else, brought into one
moment.

Now he felt something similar, but it had a different tang. As
though a perfectly ripe lemon had been squeezed onto everything. It was all more personal.

He didn't know what was true about his mom. He'd always
wanted to believe his parents' marriage had been good. That
they'd been happy.

He could no longer believe that, and, truth be told, he never
really had.

He knew his parents had often been tolerating each other—
like a business arrangement—and maybe that's why he'd clung to
Fiona the way he had. He'd wanted the perfect marriage. He'd
realized after she was gone, after it was too late, that he'd had it.
Despite the day-to-day struggles, their marriage was perfect
because they loved each other unconditionally and because it
was *theirs*.

The only one they had. The only one they'd ever have.

He didn't know if what Sy had said about his mother was
true, or if what Vellory had said was true. He didn't know, and, at
that moment, he didn't care.

He was alive. He'd already lived through the worst thing that
would ever happen to him—Fiona's murder.

All the weight of his own personal history landed in him at
that moment, and he was happy to be there. Happy in a way he
hadn't been since the moments just before he strolled out of a
midtown New York steakhouse with Fiona.

CHAPTER FORTY-FIVE

AUSTIN DIDN'T KNOW when he'd lost consciousness, but when he woke up he was on his back on the lawn behind Vellory's house.

His chest throbbed with pain and a light rain pattered his face. His ears were ringing and he heard strange noises. The wind rustled branches and carried odd calls and shouts from all directions at once. Owls and people, a barking dog. What the hell was going on?

He blinked. Sy appeared over him, staring down. He couldn't see her face. His eyes wouldn't focus all the way. But he could make out the shape of her head and her long, jet black hair.

"How'd you know I was here?" he asked.

"Anna."

"I made her promise not to tell anyone."

"You should be in the hospital."

Sy knelt, squeezed his hand. "I bounce back quick. Ambulance is on the way."

"I bounce back quick, too." Austin tried to sit up, but his body wouldn't cooperate.

"I'm not sure if you noticed, but you were shot in the chest."

Austin let out a little laugh, his chest throbbing with pain with even the slightest movement. "Thanks, I hadn't noticed." Then, suddenly, his mind pinged with a question. "Where's Vellory?"

His eyes had slowly come into focus and he saw a slight smile break across Sy's face. "I pulled your boat back to shore. He's alive. Tied up on his boat. Can't you hear him?"

Austin listened. The shouts he'd heard. They were faint and almost sounded like a TV on, far away. "That's Vellory?"

"He's not especially pleased about being tied to a boat. Lucy will be here soon. He'll be spending the night—and probably the rest of his life—in jail."

Austin used both hands to pry himself up and roll over onto his side. Pressing his knees into the ground, he slowly stood. He took off his jacket and t-shirt, allowing the light rain to hit his face. Next he pulled off the bulletproof vest and dropped it on the ground.

The rain hit his bare chest and back. Despite the pain, his legs were strong. They may have been the only part of him still uninjured. Without putting his shirt back on, he carefully slid back into his jacket and zipped it up.

Sy had been watching him. "Impressive," she said. "But you're still going to the hospital."

"That's fine. You should be going back, too."

Two police cruisers and an ambulance pulled up. Austin noticed that Mrs. Vellory was sitting on the porch wearing a white nightgown, hands folded in her lap as though all of this was perfectly normal.

Sy said, "She came out and offered me coffee while you were still passed out. She was surprised to hear that Vellory was alive."

"He put a gun in his mouth right in front of me. I think he genuinely planned to take his own life."

Sy shook her head. "And it seems like she knew."

Austin managed a weak smile. "Have you ever sat back and

thought, no matter how screwed up your life is, no matter what strange thoughts or feelings you have, no matter what odd eccentricities you have..." he thought of his parents... "or your family has... There are always stranger people out there. You ever think that?"

Sy smiled. "Thinking that is how I get through most of my days."

"I'm starving," Austin said. "There's a great 24-hour diner in Bremerton. Meet me there after the hospital?"

Paramedics were hurrying across the lawn now, clearly aiming for Austin.

"Can't," Sy said. Her voice had lost all its brightness. "They found Benny's body. Wragg had stashed it only a hundred yards from the utility shed."

"I'm sorry," Austin said.

She nodded. "I'm meeting his wife there. She has to identify the body."

"But I'll tell you what. I'll let you buy me breakfast at your place soon." She leaned in and pecked him on the cheek.

With that, she walked away and left Austin to the medics.

CHAPTER FORTY-SIX

TEN DAYS LATER, Austin again walked the half-mile trail from Twin Spits Road to the beach at Foulweather Bluff. Lucy, Ridley, and Sy had all offered to come with him, but he'd wanted to take this walk alone.

It was good that Sy hadn't been able to meet him at the diner because he'd ended up spending the night and most of the following day in the hospital. In addition to the tiny fracture in his sternum, the butt of Vellory's .45 had left his jaw misaligned. The rest of the fight had left every part of his body sore. Andy had come by and brought him a sandwich and promised to take good care of Run, as he always did when Austin was away.

The June afternoon had already hit eighty-five degrees, still milder than much of the surrounding area, but Hansville's hottest day so far that year. The well-shaded trail was a welcome respite from the heat.

He walked slower than normal as he navigated roots and branches along the trail. His chest was still wrapped with compression tape to keep it from getting reinjured, but his doctor was happy with how he was healing and he expected to be back at full strength within a month.

Anna had received all of the information Vellory had forced him to send. She'd made a weak effort to use the information to get her job back, but her boss still feared Vellory's wrath, even after he was in jail.

But things had worked out well for her. She'd used her exclusive access to the material to land a big freelance contract with a major Seattle newspaper, and published it over the last week.

Just as Vellory had said it would, the material left little doubt as to his guilt. It also showed that, while the three deceased men had been participants in the fraud, they'd made multiple objections, ultimately going along with Vellory's crimes because they'd felt they had no other choice as his subordinates.

Lucy and Daniels had spent a week arguing over jurisdiction with the Navy, and, in the end, they'd compromised. Vellory would be tried under Naval law, both for the fraud and the murders. But Perry and Maria would find justice under the authority of Kitsap County. Lucy and her team had cleared a triple homicide, which was a big deal under any circumstances. But given the weight of this particular case, it was the best possible beginning to her career as lead detective.

Ridley had texted his congratulations, but had told both Austin and Lucy that he intended to honor his suspension and not get involved in any departmental affairs. He wouldn't be back for over two and a half months.

Austin had spent much of the last ten days in bed, laptop open to the video conferencing app where the bandana-shielded face of Michael Lee had popped up not long ago. Like much of his recent life, that conversation felt surreal and far away.

To his dismay, he hadn't heard anything more from Lee.

Yesterday he'd called his friend from the NYPD, David Min-Jun, to find out if Lee had contacted him. The problem was, given the sensitivity of the case, Austin hadn't wanted to bring it up directly. And he definitely hadn't wanted to use Lee's name.

So he'd talked around it, saying things like, "What else is

going on?" and "Anything I should know about?" DMJ hadn't volunteered anything, either because he hadn't heard from Lee or because he, too, knew it was too sensitive to discuss on the phone.

In the end, Austin had decided on two things: first, he had to let Michael Lee make the next move. He'd leave his laptop open at all times in hopes that Lee would contact him again, but he wouldn't reach out. And second, he'd invite DMJ out to Hansville. His friend loved to fish, and though neither was much good at it, some of Austin's best memories had been fishing for stripers on a group charter off the coast of Connecticut at DMJ's bachelor party.

Maybe if they met in person they'd feel safe enough to talk through Lee's situation, along with how it connected to Fiona and the possibility of an investigation into the Namgung crime family. That morning, he'd tossed off an email to his friend, imploring him to make it out west before the fishing season ended.

Austin reached the end of the trail, greeted by a cool breeze drifting off the blue water.

Hammer Junior sat on a driftwood log about twenty yards away. He stood when he saw Austin.

The police tape was gone and Foulweather Bluff was back to being the pristine nature reserve Austin had visited in the past.

Hammer Junior extended a meaty hand. "Thanks for coming."

"I was honored you asked," Austin said.

In his free hand, Hammer Junior held a small ceramic urn. "My dad loved the ocean, at least that's what my mom always said. The Sound connects with the Pacific Ocean. I think this is what he would want."

Austin followed him down the beach to the shallow pools at the water line, where the clear water displayed starfish and tiny crabs. Sea anemones clung to a barnacled rock.

"Give me a minute," Hammer Junior said, kneeling in the wet sand just a few inches from the water's edge. He closed his eyes and mouthed a silent prayer.

As Austin looked out across the beach and the water, he heard the cold wind whistling on the tape Vellory had played. Sy and her team had located the original version of the recording in his house after getting a warrant. It had confirmed Austin's suspicions. The recording was real, but it had been edited.

The full conversation included a three-minute plea from Jack Hammeron and Joey Blake, begging Vellory to come clean about the fraud. They'd also wondered aloud where Adam Del Guado was, confirming that all three of them had planned to confront Vellory together, hoping their combined weight would force him to admit what he'd done. If only they'd known that Vellory was a step ahead of them.

Austin had offered to get a copy for Hammer Junior, but, oddly, he'd declined.

Austin wiped sweat from his forehead.

Hammer Junior stood and opened the urn. He waited for the breeze to die down, then slowly scattered the ashes in the water. When he was finished, he set the urn on the sand and pulled two medals from his pocket. They looked small in his large hands.

Sy had pulled some strings to have the medals released early after they'd been photographed for the file. The medals belonging to Joey Blake had been sent to his father in eastern Washington, and those of Adam Del Guado to a cousin in Florida, his closest living relative.

Hammer Junior stared at the medals for a long time. Then, reaching back, he tossed them far out into the water, where they landed with a gentle splash.

"I would have thought you'd want to keep those," Austin said.

Hammer Junior smiled sadly. "Part of me does. But in the

end, I don't want them for the same reason I didn't want to hear that recording."

"Why's that?" Austin asked as they walked back up the beach.

"I always knew my dad was good. Maybe he made some mistakes, but I always knew he was the best of the best. Even if I don't have all the memories, I have the feeling. In here." He tapped his chest. "It's hard to describe. I was three when he died, but I don't need proof. I don't need medals. Sometimes the way someone made you feel sticks with you even after the memories are gone."

Austin smiled. Hammer Junior didn't know how right he was.

When he'd spoken with his mom the day he got back from the hospital, he'd decided not to ask her about her past, about his dad, about their marriage. Sure, things had been far from perfect, but he didn't need to know. Didn't want to know.

He'd grown up feeling loved. It was more than a lot of people had and, for now, it was enough.

"I can understand that," Austin said, patting him on the back as they reached the trail.

CHAPTER FORTY-SEVEN

LUCY AND RIDLEY were laughing merrily when Austin returned. They'd pulled together the small tables in front of his store, and Jimmy was just sitting back down with a fresh pitcher of beer.

"Seems like a celebration," Austin said, pulling up a metal chair.

Ridley gave him a stern look. "Did you know about this?" He jabbed a thumb at Lucy, another at Jimmy.

Austin looked at Lucy, who shrugged. "It's okay."

Austin smiled. "I sussed out certain clues," he said, neutrally.

Jimmy poured fresh beers for everyone. "Lucy told Ridley. This is our official engagement party."

Run must have heard Austin's voice because she ran out from the shop and crashed head first into his shins, so excited she was nearly hyperventilating. He reached down and scratched behind her ears. "I'm sorry I've been gone so much." She leapt up into his lap, licked his face, sniffed at his beer for a while, then lay down for a rest.

"How's Rachel?" Austin asked.

"Uncomfortable."

Jimmy raised his beer. "To Rachel, and Rid's next child."

Everyone clanged glasses and drank.

Jimmy wiped froth from his lip. "So, boss, I mean *former* and *future* boss, is she sick of you yet. Ready for you to go back to work?"

Ridley said, "She's getting there. First few days it was great. I fixed the gutters, added some trim to the door in the laundry room, swapped out the propane tanks for the grill. Then, by day three I found myself in the kitchen, looking around and wondering, what's next?"

"You could always learn to cook," Austin offered, petting Run's head.

"Never gonna happen. I once tried to make ice cubes and screwed it up."

Lucy folded her arms. "Not possible. How?"

"Filled all the trays perfectly, but failed to close the freezer all the way. Next morning, all the ice cream was melted and I'd ruined forty bucks worth of steaks. Rachel banned me from the kitchen."

Sy's SUV pulled up and she got out, waving at the four of them and striding across the parking lot. She wore blue jeans and a white button-up and her long black hair was tied in a ponytail that stuck out the back of a Red Sox baseball hat.

Austin jogged into the store, grabbed the bouquet of flowers he'd bought that morning, and met her halfway across the parking lot. "These are for you."

She took the flowers, offering an odd, uncertain smile. "They're beautiful. Um, thanks."

Austin hadn't seen her since she visited him in the hospital the morning after he was admitted. "I, well, it's been a while, so I'll come right out with it. Do you want to have dinner with me sometime this week? I'd love to try that Italian place you mentioned."

Sy stepped back, letting the flowers drop slowly to her side. "Oh, Austin. I..."

Austin studied her eyes, uncertain.

She offered a sad smile. "Yes, let's have dinner sometime. But I have to let you know, I'm being transferred. Back to Connecticut."

She took off her hat and held it in front of him, as though the embroidered Red Sox logo was an explanation.

"You..." Austin managed. "When?"

"Three days. The good news is, I've been promoted."

"And the hat?"

"Like you, I did a few years in Connecticut back in the day. Everyone in Connecticut has to pick, Red Sox or Yankees. My husband was a Red Sox fan, so... yeah... Go Sox."

"I don't know what to say," Austin said. He was more disappointed than he wanted to admit.

Sy took his hand and led them over to the group.

For the next hour, they talked over the case, which led to past cases, which led to speculation about future cases. Sy asked Ridley whether he'd considered using his suspension to retire early, which he laughed off. He was just as addicted to the job as she was. As Austin was.

After the beer they ate burgers and drank sodas, then drank coffee and ate ice cream sandwiches. People came and went, in and out of the store buying bait, buying beer, buying sandwiches. In many ways, it was the perfect summer day in Hansville.

The sun was setting by the time Jimmy and Lucy slid their chairs away from the table. They shook hands with Sy, nodded at Ridley and Austin, and left hand in hand.

Ridley left next after picking up a gallon of milk and a jar of pickles from the store. A request Rachel had texted him during dinner.

Finally, Sy stood, then leaned in and pecked Austin on the cheek. "You're good at this job," she said.

"You are, too," Austin offered, standing to see her off.

"If you're ever in Connecticut... we'll have that dinner, or..." She trailed off, reaching out to squeeze his hand. "Goodbye, Thomas Austin."

"Bye," he said.

As he watched her leave, he felt a pang of loss, but he still felt more hopeful than he had in a long time. He smiled, tasting wilted rose petals. His chest hurt and now his heart hurt, too, though only a little. But that was better than the numbness that had lived there for nearly two years.

Run barked her quiet bark, which was designed to get his attention. When he looked over, she dropped a tennis ball on the ground, her signal that she was ready to play. He knelt down and grabbed the ball.

As he strolled to the beach, Run close on his heels, he realized that knowing Sy had changed him in a way that would take time to understand.

That was okay. He had plenty of time.

A beautiful summer lay ahead of him. A busy store, a bustling restaurant, and lots of fishing.

Austin tossed the ball as far as he could. Run bolted, kicking up sand as she raced down the beach, her back legs shooting out behind her in unison like a sprinting bunny. The water and sand were bathed in the golden glow of sunset. The feeling of peace he'd felt while staring at the dark sky on Vellory's boat had returned.

For the first time in a long time, he felt something close to content.

—The End—

Continue the Series in The Horror at Murden Cove, Book 4 of the Thomas Austin Crime Thrillers

ALSO BY D.D. BLACK

The Thomas Austin Crime Thrillers

Book 1: *The Bones at Point No Point*

Book 2: *The Shadows of Pike Place*

Book 3: *The Fallen of Foulweather Bluff*

Book 4: *The Horror at Murden Cove*

A NOTE FROM THE AUTHOR

Thomas Austin and I have three things in common. First, we both live in a small beach town not far from Seattle. Second, we both like to cook. And third, we both spend more time than we should talking to our corgis.

If you enjoyed *The Fallen of Foulweather Bluff*, I encourage you to check out the whole series of Thomas Austin novels online. Each book can be read as a standalone, although relationships and situations develop from book to book, so they will be more enjoyable if read in order.

In the digital world, authors rely more than ever on mysterious algorithms to spread the word about our books. One thing I know for sure is that ratings and reviews help. So, if you'd take the time to offer a quick rating of this book, I'd be very grateful.

If you enjoy pictures of corgis, the beautiful Pacific Northwest beaches, or the famous Point No Point lighthouse, consider joining my VIP Readers Club. When you join, you'll receive no spam and you'll be the first to hear about free and discounted eBooks, author events, and new releases.

Thanks for reading!

D.D. Black

ABOUT D.D. BLACK

D.D. Black is the author of the Thomas Austin Crime Thrillers and other Pacific Northwest crime novels that are on their way. When he's not writing, he can be found strolling the beaches of the Pacific Northwest, cooking dinner for his wife and son, or throwing a ball for his corgi over and over and over. Find out more art ddblackauthor.com, or on the sites below.

facebook.com/ddblackauthor

instagram.com/ddblackauthor

tiktok.com/@d.d.black

amazon.com/D-D-Black/e/B0B6H2XTTP

bookbub.com/profile/d-d-black